She was so over

She'd moved on and heart, in her life. He deserved nothing from her but the plate of food she slid down in front of him along with the glass of milk and the edge of contempt that welled up inside her. So why, oh why, after everything that had happened did her heart still lurch more than a little bit at the sight of his thick dark hair, his chiseled features and those amazing blue eyes?

She started to leave the table, but gasped in surprise as he grabbed her by the wrist to stop her escape…

Dear Reader,

There is nothing more pure than a mother's love, and sometimes that love requires sacrifices. In *The Cowboy's Claim,* my heroine, Courtney, comes face-to-face with the man who fathered her child, a man she believes abandoned her—and the hot, handsome cowboy wants to be an active participant in his son's life.

Sometimes as a mother we have to make choices that are difficult for us but are best for the child. I hate when that happens! Still, as Courtney chooses to do the right thing, she not only stirs up an old passion, but also a danger she'd never expected.

I hope you enjoy this book about reunion, and I hope I scare you just a little bit with the suspense.

As always, thanks for your support and keep reading!

Carla Cassidy

CARLA CASSIDY

The Cowboy's Claim

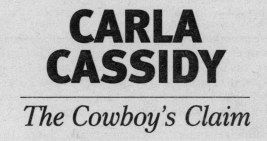

entertain, enrich, inspire™

Recycling programs
for this product may
not exist in your area.

ISBN-13: 978-0-373-27793-3

THE COWBOY'S CLAIM

www.Harlequin.com

Printed in U.S.A.

CARLA CASSIDY

is an award-winning author who has written more than one hundred books for Harlequin Books. In 1995 she won Best Silhouette Romance from *RT Book Reviews* for *Anything for Danny*. In 1998 she also won a Career Achievement Award for Best Innovative Series from *RT Book Reviews*.

Carla believes the only thing better than curling up with a good book to read is sitting down at the computer with a good story to write. She's looking forward to writing many more books and bringing hours of pleasure to readers.

Chapter 1

Nick Benson tightened his grip on the steering wheel and fought against a press of anxiety as the road sign ahead read: Grady Gulch—5 Miles.

A man wasn't supposed to feel this way when he was returning home after a two-year absence. He should be excited to connect with old friends and family, but instead each mile that took him closer to his hometown knotted the ball of anxiety in his belly tighter.

He hadn't wanted to come back to Grady Gulch, Oklahoma. In the past two years, he'd begun to slowly build a new life working as a ranch hand on an old friend's place in Texas.

Home had once been a happy place. Even though the Benson siblings had lost their parents at an early age, Nick's eldest brother, Sam, had managed not only to keep the family ranch prosperous, but he'd also kept them together as a unit. Now all of that had changed.

His sister was dead, his oldest brother was in jail and his other brother had fallen into the bottom of a bottle of booze.

His hands slowly unclenched from the steering wheel as in the distance he saw the massive billboard cowboy that topped the low, flat building of the Cowboy Café.

The café had been as much a part of Nick's life as his brothers and sister had been. On impulse, as he reached the eating establishment he pulled into the parking lot, deciding that at least he could enjoy a home-cooked meal before driving on to the family ranch and beginning to deal with the difficult issues that awaited him there.

It was just after one in the afternoon, and he'd been on the road since early morning. He'd stopped at a convenience store along the way for soda and a bag of chips, but that was all he'd eaten since leaving Texas just after dawn that morning. As he found a parking space in the lot, his stomach gave a loud rumble of anticipation.

He turned off his engine and looked at the building for a moment, remembering all the good times he and his sister and brothers had shared here. It wasn't unusual for the four of them to eat dinner together here at least twice a week.

Sam, the eldest and the most serious, played the role of parent, insisting that each of them order a side of vegetables to go with whatever else they had ordered. Adam emulated Sam, wanting to be just like the brother who was two years older than him. Meanwhile, Cherry was the one who would unscrew the top of the salt shaker just before Nick would salt his fries. She would sneak pickles off her brothers' plates and flirt shamelessly with any cowboy who walked in. By the time the meal was over, they were all laughing together. Then had come the car accident, and the laughter had died.

He shook his head as if he could dispel the very thought of the sister he had loved, the sister he had lost. There had been only two women in Nick's life who'd owned pieces of his heart, one was the sister he'd lost to death. The other he'd left behind in a fog of grief and despair.

Cherry was gone forever, but Nick had spent the past two years of his life trying to forget the other woman, and there were times in those two years he'd actually thought he'd been successful.

He finally got out of the truck and stretched with arms overhead to unkink the muscle knots that had claimed his body from hours behind the wheel. The scent of onions frying, potatoes and savory sauces filled the air, and his stomach rumbled with a new pang of hunger. Definitely time to fuel up. He had a feeling he was going to need all the strength he could muster to deal with whatever awaited him at the family ranch.

He knew that by walking into the café he'd probably be feeding the gossipmongers, but it wouldn't be the first time and it probably wouldn't be the last. Besides, might as well get it over with now, let people know he was back in town. By going inside the Cowboy Café, the word would shoot around Grady Gulch with the speed of a bullet.

As he walked into the restaurant, a little bell tinkled and he swept his black cowboy hat off his head, assuming the owner, Mary Mathis, still had her no-hats-while-eating rule in place.

Sure enough, as he looked at the wall next to the door, he saw an array of cowboy hats hanging from hooks, and he added his own to the unusual décor.

It was just late enough that the lunch rush was gone and there were only half a dozen people lingering either at the tables or at the long, polished counter.

As he made his way across the room to a booth on the other side, he was aware of several gazes following his progress. He slid into the booth and looked at the counter, where a waitress he'd never seen before poured coffee for one of the two men seated there.

He recognized one of the older men as George Wilton, the town's resident curmudgeon. George had probably been sitting at the counter since early morning, drinking coffee and complaining about anything and everything that crossed his mind. Some things never changed.

He smiled as he saw a familiar pretty blonde hurrying toward him. "Nick Benson! Well, aren't you a sight for sore eyes," Mary Mathis exclaimed.

Nick smiled at the woman who had owned the café for the past five years. "Yeah, I figured it was time I get back here and take care of some business. But before heading to the ranch, I thought I'd fill my belly with some of your food and maybe a piece of your famous pie. Sounds like I'm going to need all the strength I can muster," he said.

Mary's smile turned sympathetic. "I'm so sorry for your troubles, Nick. But, there's no question that Adam needs your help right now. The whole incident with Sam has nearly destroyed him. Rumor has it Adam is spending most of his time at The Corral, drinking himself into oblivion each night. He comes in here every once in a while looking like a broken, very hungover man."

"That's why I decided it was time to come home," Nick replied. "I could tell by the phone calls I was getting from him that things were definitely reaching a crisis point." He frowned as he thought of his older brother, who had in the past couple of weeks called him day and night, drunker than a skunk and begging him to come home.

"He needs you, Nick," Mary said, and then looked back toward the kitchen area behind the counter. "I've got to get back there. I'm teaching Junior how to make an apple pie, and if I'm not there watching his every move he'll have that pie crust turned into a smiley face. I'll send a waitress right out to take care of you."

"Thanks," Nick replied. He smiled as he thought of Junior Lempke. The shy, mentally challenged man in his mid-thirties had worked for Mary since she'd bought the place. He'd started as a busboy, with the simple task of clearing tables after diners left. It hadn't taken long for Mary to recognize that he was capable of doing more under close supervision.

It was nice to think Mary was now working with Junior to do some of the cooking. Although extremely shy and withdrawn with most people, Junior appeared not to have a mean bone in his big body.

Nick pulled the menu from where it stood between the salt and pepper shakers and opened it, although he already knew that his stomach was crying out for one of Mary's famous burgers and a side of her thick-cut, deep-fried onion rings.

What he didn't want to think about was the mess that had once been his family. Sam was in jail for attempted murder, Cherry was dead from a car accident and Adam was on an alcoholic downward spiral to disaster. Welcome home, he thought ruefully.

He sensed somebody moving to his side and looked up. He wasn't sure who radiated more stunned surprise, him or the woman clad in the black Cowboy Café

T-shirt and tight jeans, the dark-haired woman he'd spent the past two years trying to forget.

"Courtney…" Her name fell from his lips in utter shock. "Wha…what are you doing here?"

The surprise that had momentarily flittered across her pretty features was usurped by a black stare that displayed no emotion whatsoever. "What does it look like I'm doing? I'm working. Now, what can I get for you?"

Her features might not show any emotion, but he couldn't help but notice the slight tremble of her hands as she clutched an order pad and pencil.

"But why aren't you in Evanston?" he asked. Evanston was a small town almost thirty miles away where she had lived with her parents when he'd left town. He'd just assumed by now she'd be married to one of the respectable, financially well-off suitors her parents had paraded before her as potential husband material.

"I'm not in Evanston because I'm here," she replied tersely. "Are you ready to order or not?"

She was lovelier now than she'd been when they'd dated, before he'd blown out of town on a wild wind of grief. Her dark hair was longer and her features had matured from pretty to almost beautiful. She'd always been slender, but now there was a little more curve to her body.

Why was she waitressing in Grady Gulch when she could be in Evanston, where her father was the mayor and her mother ruled the social scene?

"You know, I've never stopped thinking about you," he said softly. He'd tried. God, he'd tried to forget her.

"You want a cup of coffee to go with that plate of crap?"

He sat back in the booth, as if physically thrown there by both the vitriol in her voice and the hardness that gleamed in her emerald-green eyes. For a long moment he was speechless.

"Order up or move along," she said. "I've got other customers and things to deal with."

He frowned. "I'll have a cheeseburger and onion rings and a tall glass of milk."

"Got it," she replied and then whirled away to leave the booth as if chased by the very devil himself.

Nick stared after her and wondered what had happened in the past two years that had brought her to this place in time, working as a waitress thirty miles from her hometown.

In the two years that he'd been gone, had the world gone crazy? George Wilton looked perfectly content at the counter as he finished his meal. Adam had become a drunken shadow of the man he'd once been, and the woman he'd once loved with all his heart was in a place where she didn't belong.

The worst part was he had a dreadful feeling this was just the beginning, that things were going to get crazier before they got better. He'd better prepare himself for more surprises that lie ahead.

Courtney Chambers placed Nick's order with Rusty the cook and then sank down in a chair in the kitchen area, her legs shaking so hard she might never walk again.

She should have expected that he'd eventually come back home, especially after Sam and Adam's recurrent plunge into despair. And she should have expected that if he did come back to Grady Gulch, he'd eventually make his way back into the Cowboy Café.

But she hadn't been expecting it to be today, and in the very depths of her heart she'd hoped she'd never see him again. Just looking into the brightness of his blue eyes had brought back all the heartbreak, all the anguish he'd left behind when he'd disappeared from Grady Gulch without a word on the day that his sister had been buried.

She'd loved him as she'd never loved another man, had given herself to him and only him with the notion that eventually they'd get married and raise a family together. And then he'd disappeared and she'd never heard from him again.

She straightened in her chair as Mary touched her shoulder. "Are you okay?" Mary looked at her worriedly.

"I'm fine," Courtney said with forced reassurance. The last thing she wanted to do was bother her boss, the woman who had been equal parts employer and surrogate mother to her for the past two years.

"Are you sure?" Mary raised a pale blond eyebrow.

"I'm good. Just resting my feet for a minute or two while Rusty gets my order ready," she replied, knowing that it was very rare she simply sat to wait for an order.

Mary eyed her skeptically for a long moment and then nodded and moved back to where she had been working with Junior. Courtney sighed in relief. She didn't want to lie to Mary, who had been so good to her, but she also didn't want anyone to know how badly seeing Nick again had affected her. She'd thought she was emotionally dead where he was concerned, but she was apparently wrong.

"Order up," Rusty said, and Courtney reluctantly got to her feet, knowing she'd have to look at *him* again. She filled a big glass with milk and then grabbed the plate from the pass window and headed back to the booth where Nick sat.

Why hadn't he gotten obese in the two years since

she'd last seen him? Why hadn't he grown a beer belly and jowls? Why hadn't that charming cleft in his chin fallen off his handsome face? Or his broad shoulders turned to toothpicks?

Why, oh why, after everything that had happened, did her heart still lurch more than a little bit at the sight of his thick dark hair, his chiseled features and those amazing blue eyes?

She was so over him. She'd moved on, and he had no place in her heart, in her life. He deserved nothing from her but the plate of food she slid down in front of him along with the glass of milk and the edge of contempt that welled up inside her.

She started to leave the table but gasped in surprise as he grabbed her by the wrist to stop her escape. "It isn't that busy," he said. "Why don't you sit with me for a minute or two?"

"Why would I want to do that?" she replied as she pulled her wrist from his grasp. Her need to escape was overwhelming, but she didn't want him to see that he bothered her in any way, that he still had any power at all over her.

"I don't know. I thought maybe we could catch up a little bit."

"Why?" She forced a light laugh. "I mean honestly, Nick, what on earth would we have to talk about? You've been gone for two years. We've both moved on with our lives."

He studied her intently, and she kept her features carefully schooled so as not to display any of the turmoil that twirled around in her stomach. "I should have called you," he finally said.

Her stomach clenched. "Yes, you should have," she agreed. "But, you didn't, and time went by and life went on. It's all water under the bridge. Now, is there anything else I can get for you?"

"Not at the moment," he replied after a long hesitation.

She turned and left the booth, but she was aware of his gaze lingering on her, heating the center of her back. She escaped back to the safety of the kitchen and once again pasted a smile on her lips.

Instead of keeping Nick Benson in her mind, she thought of Grant Hubert, the man she'd been dating for the past two months.

Grant was everything Nick hadn't been…dependable and mature. He was thirty-five, the vice president of the local bank, and he'd been the first man she'd allowed into her life in any way since Nick.

Grant didn't stir in her the same crazy emotions that Nick had once evoked. Instead he felt solid and predictable, and that was exactly what she needed in her life at this moment.

She knew what had brought Nick back to town, but the Bensons weren't the only ones who had gone through trauma in the past couple of months.

Certainly everyone had been shocked when Sam Benson had tried to kill Courtney's friend and fellow waitress, Lizzy Wiles, but before that the entire town had been equally shocked when another waitress from the café had been brutally murdered.

That murder had not yet been solved and hadn't been related to Sam's attack on Lizzy. At the time, Courtney, Lizzy and Candy, the murdered young woman, had been living in three of the four little cottages just behind the café.

It had been Candy's murder and the attack on Lizzy that had prompted Sheriff Cameron Evans to arrange for

Courtney to move from the cottage to a nearby motel. In the past two months the motel room, with its kitchenette, had finally begun to feel like home.

Thankfully, when she returned to the booth where Nick had sat enough money to pay his tab and a generous tip for her was all that remained.

She rang up his order, pocketed her tip and told herself she absolutely refused to spend another minute of her time thinking about Nick Benson. Besides, there was plenty to do to prepare for the evening dinner rush. That would keep her mind sufficiently occupied.

Since the time she'd moved to Grady Gulch, she'd come to love the people of the small town. Even George Wilton, who complained about the bitterness of the coffee, the dryness of the meat loaf and the laziness of today's youth, held a certain charm all his own.

The dinner rush that evening seemed busier than usual, and despite her desire not to think about Nick Benson, he seemed to be the topic of conversation on everyone's lips.

"They've all come to bad ends," Susan Walker said to her husband as Courtney served them the nightly special. "One dead, one a convict, one a drunk, and Nick always was a bit of a hellion." She shook her head ruefully. "Guess that's what happens to kids when their parents die too young."

"All of them spent too much time down at The Corral," David Bentz said to his wife as Courtney delivered their drinks to their table. "I heard through the grapevine that Nick has come back to somehow save Adam from himself." David snorted. "That's kind of like the pot calling the kettle to ask for advice."

Courtney grimaced, fighting the impulse to say something in defense of all the Bensons. She'd never liked David Bentz much anyway. He always smelled just a little bit like cow manure.

"How are you doing tonight, Courtney?" Abigail Swisher asked as Courtney stopped at her table.

"Good. And where's that handsome husband of yours?" she asked. It was unusual for Abigail to show up at the café without her husband, Fred.

"He's on a business trip, and I decided I didn't feel like cooking tonight. The house was just too darned quiet." Abigail gave her a sweet smile and swept a strand of her light brown hair behind an ear. Courtney caught a pleasant scent of spring flowers wafting from the woman.

"Good for you," Courtney replied. She knew the couple didn't have children. Abigail had suffered a miscarriage, but rumor had it they were trying desperately for another child.

She took Abigail's order, and by the time the dinner rush was over Courtney was sick of hearing all the negative stories about Nick—and even more sick that in each case she'd wanted to somehow jump to his defense.

It was after eight when Courtney finally sat down to take a break with fellow waitress Lynette Shiver. Lynette was twenty-three and had been working at the café for only about a month.

She'd been hired when Lizzy had quit her job as a waitress to move in with her future husband, Daniel Jefferson. Lizzy seemed perfectly content helping Daniel around the ranch and planning a wedding for the near future.

"Would you please tell me about the Benson family?" Lynette exclaimed. "That's all I've heard about all night, and I didn't know what anyone was talking about. Sounds like a nice plate of juicy gossip."

"It's actually a tragic story on several levels," Courtney replied with a sigh of resignation. As much as she hadn't wanted to talk about Nick, she knew there was no way she could avoid the topic while explaining to Lynette what had happened before she'd come to the small town.

"The Benson family consisted of Sam, who was the eldest, Adam, Cherry and Nick. Their parents died years ago, and Sam took the reins of the family ranch and worked hard to keep them all together. Then two years ago Cherry was killed in a car accident."

Courtney took a sip of her iced tea and tried not to remember that night. She'd been in her bedroom in her parents' house and had gotten a text from Nick to meet him at the place where they always rendezvoused away from prying eyes.

When she'd finally gotten to the old Yates place, she'd driven past the old house that had been foreclosed on years ago and never resold and drove straight down the lane that took her to the old barn.

Nick's pickup was already there, and when she entered the horse stall that had been their special place for the past seven months, he'd grabbed her and pulled her to him as he wept.

They'd made love, silently, emotionally, and then he'd left the barn without saying a word. She'd known his grief was too great for words, and she'd let him go that night assuming they'd have time together the next day or the day after that. And then he was gone from Grady Gulch, from her.

"Earth to Courtney." Lynette's voice pulled her away from the painful memories.

"Sorry. Anyway, Cherry was killed, along with Daniel Jefferson's wife, Janice. Rumor had it that Daniel and Janice had a fight and Janice called Cherry to pick her up. The two left the Jefferson place, it was snowing and Cherry was driving way too fast. They crashed, and both women were killed."

"That's definitely tragic," Lynette said as she raised her coffee cup to her lips.

Courtney nodded. "Daniel was real torn up about it, and so was Sam. But what nobody knew was that Sam blamed Daniel for his sister's death. Daniel was a broken man, but then he met Lizzy, who was working as a waitress here, and the two of them fell in love. Sam went crazy and tried to kill Lizzy because she made Daniel happy, and in Sam's distraught mind Daniel wasn't allowed to ever be happy again as long as Cherry was gone."

"So, Sam was caught and arrested and Adam's acting like the town drunk, and now it sounds like Nick has ridden to the rescue, coming home to take care of things."

"Something like that," Courtney replied, tired of the Benson family drama and still reeling from the fact that Nick was back in town.

Minutes later, Mary walked over to where the two of them sat. "Thursday nights are usually slow. Is one of you up for going home early?"

Lynette waved her hand to Courtney. "Go on. I know you have important places to be and people to see. I'll close it up tonight."

Courtney breathed a deep sigh. "Thanks, Lynette. I wouldn't mind getting off a little early this evening."

"Then go, get on out of here," Mary said. "Lynette and I can handle things for the rest of the night."

Courtney didn't wait for Mary to change her mind. She quickly got up from her chair and carried her cup to the counter. "I'm out of here," she said as she headed toward the front door. "I'll see you at noon tomorrow."

She caught her breath as she stepped out into the hot July night. As she walked to her car, the heat that had been trapped in the asphalt all day long radiated up to her tired feet. She couldn't wait to get home to the motel, kick off her shoes and just relax. But she had one more important stop to make.

She always sent up a silent prayer when she got behind the wheel of her car and turned the key. Thankfully her prayer was answered and the engine turned over. She'd bought the car dirt cheap because she had more important things to spend her money on than transportation.

She sat for a minute, allowing the interior of the car to begin to cool from the air conditioner, before heading to Sophie Martinez's home.

She consciously tried to keep her mind blank as she drove the distance to the attractive little ranch house situated on several acres just outside the city limits. She was tired of thinking of the past and wanted only to focus on the future.

Tomorrow night she had a dinner date with Grant, and she was off work all day Saturday and Sunday. She always looked forward to spending time with Grant and some downtime on the weekends.

At the moment she didn't feel the anticipation that a date with Grant usually brought, and she hated the fact that a simple interaction with Nick had somehow managed to throw her off.

She shoved every thought in her head away as she pulled down the long lane that led to Sophie's ranch house. This was the moment each day that she looked forward to most, arriving here after hours of being separated from the most important person in her life.

Her tired feet nearly danced to the front door, where she knocked softly. The door opened and Sophie greeted her with a surprised smile. "Courtney, you're a bit early tonight."

"We weren't too busy so Mary let me go for the night."

Sophie opened the door to allow her into the neat living room with modest furnishings. Sophie was a young widow with two small children. Thankfully there had been enough insurance money to allow her not only to keep her house and the surrounding land but also stay at home with her two little daughters for the next couple of years.

For extra money she had become a licensed day care provider, and her family room off the kitchen had been turned into a kid's playland.

From that room a cacophony of sound escaped. It was the happy chaos of children at play… The squeals of little girls, the laughter of little boys and the squawk of the cockatiel that hung in a cage on a large stand near the window.

"Sounds like you have a full house this evening," Courtney said as they headed toward the family room. Usually by the time Courtney arrived there was only one or two extra children.

"The Morrises asked if I could keep the twins late tonight. It's their anniversary and they wanted to have a nice romantic evening together without the boys," Sophie explained.

As they entered the family room, Courtney's gaze automatically darted around the room for the fifteen-month-old dark-haired, blue-eyed little boy who owned her heart and soul.

Garrett. He was clad in a pair of cowboy-printed pajamas and sat on the floor playing with a stack of colorful wooden blocks. When Courtney drew closer, he looked up and his face was wreathed in smiles.

"Ma-Ma!" He raised his chubby little arms toward her.

As she picked him up, her heart swelled full in her chest. "Hi, baby. Hi, Garrett," she said as she kissed the side of his face. "Were you a good boy today for Sophie?"

"Sophie," he echoed and pointed to his daily caretaker.

"He's always a good boy when he's here. He's the most laid-back toddler I've ever met. He's freshly changed and ready for bed."

Courtney smiled and gave Garrett a hug. "Thanks, Sophie. We'll get out of your hair, and I'll see you tomorrow around eleven-thirty."

Sophie walked with her to the door, and a minute later Courtney had Garrett in his car seat in the back of the car. By the time she arrived at the motel, he was fast asleep.

She gently lifted him from the seat and carried him into the motel room they called home. Next to her bed was the crib, where she gently placed the sleeping boy and covered him with a light blanket. She laid her finger lightly on his little cleft chin, as if wanting to hide the characteristic that marked his paternity.

For several long moments she gazed at the son who had been conceived the night of Cherry Benson's death. That night, as Nick had come at her with silent, horrible grief and she'd embraced him, needing to somehow ease his pain, neither of them had thought about birth control.

And when Nick had blown out of town, he'd had no idea that he'd left her with a piece of him that would change her life forever.

He hadn't called. He'd offered no explanation. He'd just disappeared. And now it was too late. He had left her without a word, broken all the promises they'd made to each other. He didn't deserve to have a son, and she had no intention of ever telling him of Garrett's existence.

Chapter 2

The Benson ranch had always been a source of great pride. Not only had it been financially successful, but Sam had worked hard to keep the large ranch house, surrounding lawn and outbuildings in pristine condition.

As Nick got his first glimpse of home, his heart dropped to his feet as he realized it was far worse than what he'd expected. Despite the summer heat, the lawn was a jungle of overgrown weeds and brush. A tractor-style mower sat amid the mess, as if at some point the operator had simply given up on any attempt to restore order.

Nick got out of his truck, momentarily overwhelmed by the neglect around him. Obviously Cherry's death had yielded far-reaching effects that none of them could have ever foreseen.

For just a minute Nick wanted to jump back into his truck and drive as fast as he could back to his uncomplicated life in Texas. Run…avoid…escape painful and difficult things. That's what he'd done on the day of Cherry's funeral. But, that was the man he'd been two years ago. That wasn't the man he was now.

Straightening his shoulders, he headed for the stairs leading up to the front porch, noting that one of the handrails was missing.

He opened the front door and his nose was instantly assailed by the odors of overripe fruit, dirty socks and sour booze.

"Hello?" he called. "Adam…are you here?"

"In the kitchen," a deep voice returned.

Nick found his older brother seated at the kitchen table, his fingers curled around a coffee mug and his bloodshot blue eyes narrowed to near slits. "So, the prodigal son has finally come home." There was a touch of censure in Adam's voice that Nick ignored.

As Nick went to the cabinet to grab a mug, he tried to ignore the mound of dirty dishes in the sink and the garbage bag that overflowed onto the floor. "Is that coffee fresh?"

Adam nodded. "I made it about an hour ago when I finally decided to get out of bed."

Nick poured his coffee and then sat in the chair opposite his brother. "Been spending a lot of time in bed?"

"In bed or drunk." Adam raised his chin as if in defiance.

"Sounds productive." Nick took a sip of the strong coffee and held his brother's gaze above the rim of his cup. Adam was thirty-three, but at the moment he looked ten years older.

"You should have been here, Nick." Adam finally broke the gaze and instead stared at some point over Nick's shoulder. "You should have stuck around after

Cherry died, then maybe you would have seen the sickness in Sam, the sickness I didn't see."

Nick sat back in his chair, surprised as he continued to look at his brother. "Surely you aren't blaming yourself for what Sam has done?"

Adam raked a hand through his thick, dark, unruly hair. "I should have seen that he was sick, that he was howl-at-the-moon crazy. He and I were so close. If I'd known how he felt I might have been able to stop him. But somehow I missed something, and now there's nothing left of our family. Cherry is gone, Sam has disgraced us all and there's nothing left."

"There's you and me," Nick replied. "Adam, you've got to pull yourself up out of this funk and get back to the job of taking care of this place, taking care of yourself."

Adam shoved back from the table. "I don't want to hear you telling me what I have to do. You ran out on us. I figure you'll be here for a week or two and when you realize how tough it is to live in a small town where everyone's talking about your family, when things get just a little bit too hard, then you'll do what you always do—you'll run out again. Now, if you'll excuse me, I have a bottle of whiskey waiting for me in my room."

As Adam left the kitchen, Nick remained at the table. Yes, it was definitely worse than he thought. He and Adam had never been particularly close. Sam had been thirty-four and Adam thirty-one when Nick had left town. The two older brothers had always aligned with each other, while Cherry and Nick had bonded together as the younger siblings.

He finished his coffee, rinsed his cup and then went outside, deciding the dishes and the other kitchen cleanup could wait until later. He headed for the stables in the distance, wanting to ride the pastures and check out the livestock.

Surely Adam hadn't fallen so deep into the bottom of the bottle and his depression that he hadn't been feeding and caring for the horses and the cattle that provided their livelihood.

He sighed in relief as he walked into the stable and saw that all the horses were in good shape. It took him only minutes to saddle up his old mount, Diamond, and head to the distant pastures.

As he rode with the heat of the sun on his shoulders, he finally began to relax, but he couldn't help the way his thoughts went back to Courtney. He'd been so shocked to see her working in the café.

As the horse rocked him in the saddle, he thought of the last time they'd been together. It had been hours after he'd learned that his sister had died, and he'd needed Courtney's warmth, her life force and energy to take away the icy-cold grip of grief.

When he'd left Grady Gulch on the day of Cherry's funeral, he had no plans to stay away for as long as he had. It had just happened. Days turned into weeks, weeks into months, and suddenly two years had passed.

A hundred times…no, maybe a thousand times in the time he'd been gone, he'd stared at his cell phone and mentally punched in Courtney's number, just wanting to hear the sound of her voice, to feel some sort of connection with her.

For months after he'd left Grady Gulch, Courtney had been like the phantom limb of an amputee. But with each day that had passed, it had gotten a little easier to stop himself from contacting her.

After all, he'd always been her dirty little secret, a walk on the wild side that she'd kept private from everyone in her life. The promises they'd made to each other to love one another forever, to eventually marry and have a family together, had been nothing more than silly fantasies they'd spin in moments of happy delusion and sexual satisfaction. The promises, the love, all of it had never left the abandoned Yates barn.

She had been the princess of Evanston, and he'd been the bad-boy cowboy from Grady Gulch, never welcomed to her home, never even introduced to her family or friends, but rather hidden in the shadows of the old barn.

He pushed Diamond a little harder as a slight edge of anger rose up inside him. He'd wanted so much more from Courtney, but she'd been so afraid of what her parents would think, so worried about how the people of her hometown would react if she hooked up with one of the wild Benson brothers who were and always would be nothing more than ranching cowboys.

Consciously shoving thoughts of Courtney out of his mind, he breathed a sigh of relief as he saw the herd of cattle in the distance. Even from this vantage point he could tell they looked healthy and happy. At least Adam had been tending the livestock, even if he hadn't been tending to himself.

He turned his horse around and headed back to the house. Adam was still holed up in his bedroom, and Nick didn't bother trying to get him out.

The drive from Texas, along with the stress of seeing both Courtney and the neglected house, had exhausted him. He took a long hot shower, and even though it was early, he went to the bedroom that had been his before he'd left town.

Although his intention was just to rest for a while and then get up and get some work done, he fell into a deep sleep. His dreams were of Courtney and the magical seven months they'd spent together. Laughter, love-making and spinning fantasies had filled their time.

He awoke with the morning light, the faint taste of bitterness and regret in his mouth. He'd known from the beginning that she wasn't his to keep; there had just been moments in the past when he'd forgotten that fact.

Adam wasn't up yet and Nick had a feeling he wouldn't be for some time, so around seven Nick headed for the Cowboy Café and a hearty breakfast to start his day. As he drove he thought about the dreams he'd had the night before and reminded himself that Courtney was nothing more than a piece of his past.

It was about seven-fifteen when he pulled into the café parking lot. There were only a few other diners that early in the morning. It took him a quick glance around to see that Courtney wasn't one of the wait-resses working.

Good. He could eat his breakfast without feeling her animosity toward him, without thoughts of her disturbing his appetite.

He slid onto a stool at the counter and smiled at Mary, who stood behind it wiping it down with a clean cloth. "Start you off with some coffee, Nick?"

"Sounds perfect," he replied and watched as she set the cleaning cloth aside, washed her hands in the sink and then poured him a cup of the fragrant fresh brew.

"How was the homecoming?" she asked. Mary Mathis was an attractive woman with blond hair and clear blue eyes. She had a ten-year-old son named Matt, who was obviously her heart. He'd never heard of her dating anyone, even though she was a widow who had shown up in town eight years ago.

"A bit tense," he admitted. "The house was a mess, but I think my brother is a bigger mess."

"One way or another, things will eventually straighten themselves out. They always do," she said with her usual optimism. "At least you're home now and can maybe help Adam find his way back to the land of the living."

"He definitely hasn't shown any signs of being alive or even wanting to resurface since I arrived," Nick replied drily.

"He's a strong man. He's just lost his way a little bit. This thing with Sam definitely shook him up. Now, what can I get you for breakfast?"

Nick ordered the classic café combo of eggs, bacon and a buttermilk biscuit, and a stack of pancakes on the side. He figured he would need all the fuel he could handle to then head back to the ranch and start figuring things out. The ranch needed work and somehow he had to get Adam's head back in the game of life.

He was halfway through his meal when George Wilton came in and slid onto the stool next to him at the counter. "About time you came home," he said to Nick. "Your family is falling apart."

"So I've heard."

"Are you home to stay?"

"Doubtful," Nick said truthfully. "Although I imagine I'll be here through the fall."

"Rumor has it you've been working in Texas."

"The rumor is true." Nick knifed butter over his pancakes as Mary approached to get George's order.

"Speaking of rumors, I just heard that another waitress from the café was murdered last night," the old man said. Both Mary and Nick stared at him. "I can guess by the look on your faces that the sheriff hasn't been in here yet this morning."

"Who?" The single word yanked from Nick's throat with a hoarse despair. "Who was murdered?"

"I don't know. The sheriff didn't reveal her name. I just met him as I was leaving my house."

Nick looked at Mary, whose face had blanched of all color. "Is Courtney here now?"

She shook her head. "She works a short shift today, noon to five. I've got five waitresses who aren't in."

That made it five to one that the murdered waitress could be Courtney. Nick's heart banged hard, leaving him half-breathless with fear.

At that moment Sheriff Cameron Evans walked through the door. His stern features softened as he looked at Mary. "I guess you've heard. We have another one."

It had been their usual date. Grant was pleasant, as was the conversation that flowed easily between the two of them. Everything was so uncomplicated with Grant. He was the perfect gentleman and always made Courtney feel at ease, unlike Nick, who felt like an out-of-control tornado that whirled through her body and mind each time he was in sight.

"Terrible thing about Shirley Cook," Grant said as they lingered over coffee. "I heard she was killed the same way Candy Bailey was… In bed with her throat cut."

Courtney wrapped her fingers around her coffee mug, seeking warmth as she thought of the unsolved murders. "Sheriff Evans was in and out of the café all afternoon, interviewing each of us to see if we might know who Shirley was seeing, if anybody was giving her problems or anything that might point in the direction of a potential killer."

"Were you able to give him any information?" Grant asked, his brown eyes sympathetic. He was a nice-looking man with light brown hair and mildly hand-some features.

He didn't make her heart beat any faster. He didn't stir the crazy passion that Nick always had. But that was okay. What she needed most in her life right now was stable and responsible, and it was ironic that Grant was that kind of man with the kind of job that her parents would have approved of.

"No, I couldn't help him at all," she replied to his question. "Shirley was a bit older than me. We didn't run in the same crowd and didn't socialize much at work and not at all outside of work. She was a quiet woman who minded her own business and always showed up for work on time."

A bubble of grief welled up inside Courtney's throat as she thought of the woman who had died before her time, died so violently…like Candy before her.

"Have you considered quitting your job?"

She looked at him in surprise. "Why would I do that?"

He shrugged. "Two women murdered and both were waitresses at the Cowboy Café. What if somebody is specifically targeting the women who work there?"

"Sheriff Evans thinks it's more likely that maybe Kevin Naperson killed both women." Kevin had been Candy Bailey's boyfriend at the time of her murder, and despite the fact that his father had given him an alibi for that night, Courtney knew he'd never dropped off the top of the suspect list for Candy's murder.

"Kill another woman who he has no ties with and take the heat off himself for Candy's murder. It's an in-teresting theory." Grant picked up his coffee cup and took a sip, then carefully set the mug back on the table in the precise position it had been in originally.

"Either that or somebody else is a killer and both women were vulnerable," she replied.

"And you don't feel vulnerable?" Grant asked with a quirk of his neatly trimmed eyebrow.

She gave him a rueful smile. "I live in a motel, Grant. There are nights I hear somebody drop their soap in their shower, or the snoring of a man who has rented the unit next door for a night. I feel perfectly safe there. I'm completely surrounded by people."

"You know, I could arrange for you to be in another place…a better place for you and Garrett. All you have to do is ask me."

"I know, but really we're fine where we are." She wasn't at a place in her relationship with Grant that she wanted any favors from him. She wanted to be beholden to nobody, taking care of herself as she should have years ago. "And it's probably time for me to go pick up Garrett. I told Sophie before we left that it wouldn't be a late night."

"Then let's go pick up the munchkin," he agreed easily.

Within half an hour they were at Courtney's room at the motel. "You want to come in for one last cup of coffee?" she asked as she held a sleeping Garrett in her arms.

"Sure, that would be great," he readily agreed.

It had become their routine on Friday nights after dinner for him to come into the motel room and share a cup of coffee before he headed home.

She never worried about things getting intimate. So far their physical relationship had consisted of a couple of chaste kisses when they said good-night.

With Garrett to consider, she'd been reluctant to date anyone, but Grant had been persistent and she'd finally agreed to go out with him with the understanding that things between them would go slow. He'd respected her wishes, and their romance, such as it was, had progressed at a snail's pace.

With Garrett soundly sleeping in his crib and coffee made, they sat across from each other at the tiny table under the single hanging light in the room and talked about the hot weather, the plans the town had for a summer festival in the next couple of weeks and their own plans to enjoy that day together.

"The bank is sponsoring a stand offering free soda and bottled water, and I'm assigned to work it from nine to eleven that day. But after eleven I'll be all yours," Grant said in the soft voice he always used so as not to awaken the sleeping child.

"Sounds like it's going to be a wonderful day, although it doesn't seem right to be looking forward to a festival with two unsolved murders in the town." As she thought of Shirley's murder, she fought off a shiver that threatened to waltz up her spine.

"We just have to stay focused on the positive," Grant replied. "Sheriff Evans is a good man and he'll figure out these crimes eventually."

"I hope so," she said fervently.

Even though she was hoping that it was mere coincidence that both Candy and Shirley had worked at the café, there was no question the fact that two of her coworkers had been murdered unnerved her more than just a little bit.

Grant glanced at his watch. "I'd better get out of here. I have to go into the bank early tomorrow." He got up from the table and carried his empty cup to the sink.

"Thank you, as always, for a lovely evening," Courtney said as she walked him to the door.

He kissed her on the forehead, the scent of his expensive cologne a bit overpowering. "I'll call you tomorrow?"

"I'd like that," she agreed. "The only thing I have planned is maybe taking Garrett to the city park, but I'll probably wait until early evening when it cools down a bit."

He frowned. "Take a friend with you. I don't like the idea of you out and around all alone, especially if you plan on being out after dark."

She smiled, touched by his concern. "Don't worry, I'll be back here long before dark."

They murmured their goodbyes, and then he left and Courtney carefully locked the door behind him. She'd just carried her cup to the sink when a knock fell on her door.

As she hurried to answer she assumed it was Grant who had either left something behind or had forgotten to tell her something.

She unlocked the door and pulled it open to see Nick leaning casually against the doorjamb. "What on earth are you doing here?" she asked in surprise, praying that Garrett stayed asleep and quiet in his crib.

"Is that who you're dating now? Grant Hubert?" he asked, as if he had a right to know anything about her or who she might be seeing.

"That's really none of your business." She stepped outside and pulled the door halfway closed behind her so that he couldn't see into the room.

"Your parents must be so proud of you. Grant has a good position with the bank, a real air of respectability about him. Is that why you moved here? To be closer to him?" Although his features betrayed nothing, his voice held just the faintest edge of resentment.

"Exactly what part of 'it's none of your business' don't you understand? And I'll repeat it again, what are you doing here?"

"Can I come in for a minute?"

"Absolutely not," she replied and tightened her grip on the doorknob of the half-closed door. The last thing in the world she wanted was for this man to know about his son.

Garrett didn't need him in his life. Garrett didn't need a man who had left her without a backward glance, a man who would probably blow back out of town again before too long.

"I heard about the murder of the waitress this morning, and about the other murder before that," he said. In the shadows of the night the cleft in his chin looked deeper than usual and his eyes appeared almost black. "I guess I just wanted to stop by and see that you were okay."

"As you can see, I'm just fine." Even though she wanted to feel nothing for him, she couldn't help the way her heart squeezed slightly at the thought that he might care about her just a little.

Not that she cared about him anymore. She'd stopped caring about Nick Benson in the weeks after he'd left when he hadn't even bothered to call her, when he hadn't thought her worth any kind of an explanation of why he had left. She'd stopped caring about Nick Benson when he'd shattered her world by walking away without even a backward glance.

"You look good, Courtney," he said, his gaze appearing soft in the moonlight. His gaze slid down the length of her. "You look real good."

At that moment a cry came from inside the room. Apparently Garrett had awakened. Nick's features froze as Courtney's heart crashed to the ground.

"That yours?" he asked, his voice flat.

"It is." Her heart beat fast and furious in her chest.

"So, I guess you've really moved on."

"What did you expect? That I'd pine away just because you were gone? I've got to go." Before he could say anything else she slid back into the room and closed the door, then leaned against it and prayed he wouldn't ask anyone exactly when Garrett had been born.

Mary Mathis sat across a café table from Sheriff Cameron Evans. He almost always ended his nights here, drinking the last of the coffee after she closed the restaurant.

He was a handsome man, with dark brown hair and hazel eyes that changed with his mood. Tonight they were more brown than green, and his eyebrows were pulled down into a frown.

"It's just like Candy's murder," he said as he wrapped his big, strong fingers around his coffee mug. "No forensic evidence, no obvious suspect."

"What about Kevin Naperson?" Mary asked, knowing he'd been the main suspect when Candy had been killed.

"I spoke to him first thing this morning and his alibi is that he was in bed asleep, which is going to be pretty much the same alibi of everyone in the entire town. We've fixed Shirley's time of death at 3:12 a.m."

Mary raised an eyebrow. "That's pretty specific."

Cameron nodded. "Apparently while the killer was attacking Shirley he managed to pull the cord to her clock radio out of the wall. That's the time the clock stopped."

An edge of grief stabbed through Mary, along with a whisper of fear. It was a fear she could share with nobody, the fear that somehow this was all happening because of her, because of her past sins.

"You okay?" Cameron looked at her with concern.

"Yes and no," she admitted. "I'm trying not to make this personal, but two of my waitresses have been brutally murdered."

"There's absolutely no reason to believe this is about you or the café. Right now we just happen to have two victims who coincidentally worked at the same place. Let's not make it bigger than it is."

For one heart-stopping moment she thought he might reach over and touch her, maybe cover her hand with his big, strong one, and for just an aching moment of weakness, she wanted him to.

It seemed like a lifetime that she'd felt even the most simple touch from a man, and of all the men in town, Cameron was the one who made her heart beat just a little faster whenever he was around.

Instead, he rose to his feet with a weary sigh. "I've got to get back to work. As always, thanks for the coffee and the moment of sanity in my day."

She smiled and rose to her feet, as well. "It's after midnight. You should just go home and straight to bed and start fresh in the morning."

"You're right, but that isn't what I'm going to do. I'm heading back to the crime scene at Shirley's house to see what we might have missed earlier."

He lingered at the door, and for a moment she wanted to fall into the softness she saw in his eyes as he gazed at her. "Lock up after me and I'll see you in the morning." With another deep sigh, he left the café.

She locked the door and then shut off the last of the lights in the café. She walked through the kitchen and to a door that led to the area of the building she and her son called home.

There was a nice-size living room with a bedroom on each side. Matt had the bigger of the two bedrooms and at the moment was sound asleep in his bed.

She stood in his doorway and watched him, her heart expanding with love. Everything she had done, she'd done for him. Every bad thing she'd ever accomplished, every lie she'd ever told, had all been in an effort to save Matt.

And she'd succeeded. He was a happy, healthy young boy who had no memory of the first two years of his life. And for that she would forever be grateful. He didn't suffer the kind of nightmares she did from those years. He slept peacefully, as the young and innocent should sleep.

She moved from his room across the living room to her smaller bedroom. Lately it seemed that every night her sleep was disturbed by nightmares. And recently she'd been dreaming not only about the crime that had taken place so many years before, but also about Candy's murder. Now she had Shirley's terrible death to add to her landscape of nightmares.

Minutes later, as she slid beneath the sheet and turned off the light next to her bed, she tried to focus on what Cameron had said to her—don't take it personally.

She hoped that what people were speculating about Kevin Naperson was true. He'd always been the number one suspect in Candy Bailey's murder. Maybe he'd killed Shirley to take the heat off himself, to make it look as if there was some crazy serial killer in the town offing waitresses.

Or perhaps it truly was just a strange coincidence that both murdered women worked at the café. Mary had twelve women working various shifts, both full-time and part-time, at the restaurant. Grady Gulch was a small town where many women didn't work outside their homes.

She closed her eyes, determined to get to sleep despite everything that whirled through her head. Her flighty thoughts landed and stayed on Cameron Evans.

He'd made it clear in all kind of ways that he'd like to pursue something romantic with her. Matt adored the sheriff, and there were times Mary longed for nothing more than his big, strong arms around her, that she would love to invite him into her life, into her heart.

But the choices she had made long ago would forever keep her alone. And if by some chance Cameron discovered the truth of who she was and what she had done, he wouldn't love her, he'd arrest her.

Chapter 3

She had a child.

The fact had haunted Nick throughout the night, and when he awakened the next morning it was with the same thought in his mind. Courtney had a baby.

When had it happened? Did the baby belong to Grant Hubert? Is that why she was living and working in Grady Gulch? So her baby could be close to his father? If that was the case, then why weren't the two of them already married?

And just how old was the baby? How quickly did Courtney move on after Nick had left town?

What he couldn't understand was why the idea bothered him so much. She'd been right. He had no business asking her questions about the choices she'd made after he'd left here. He'd lost the right to know anything about her personal life when he'd decided to disappear.

But knowing that didn't stop the small pang in his

heart as he thought of her having a child with another man. He was supposed to have been the father of her children.

Often when they'd spent time together in the Yates barn they'd talked about their future together. They both wanted children, a little boy first and then a girl. They'd buy a ranch and build a family. That had been their dream, but even as they'd talked about it, deep in his heart Nick had always known that it was all just foolish fantasy.

Even when she was twenty-four years old, Courtney's parents had, for the most part, been running her life, making all the important decisions for her. Their princess daughter marrying a Benson boy and becoming a rancher's wife had not been part of their master plan. Courtney had been so afraid of disappointing her parents, the relationship she and Nick had shared had been conducted undercover.

He shoved all thoughts of Courtney and her baby out of his mind as he drank two cups of coffee and then headed outside to see if he could make some headway on the lawn.

He reminded himself he wasn't here to reconnect with Courtney in any way. He was here to pull Adam up from his depression and get the ranch back in good shape. That was all, and that was more than enough. Once he'd done what he'd come to do, he'd hightail it back to his own life in Texas.

The sun was already hot overhead as he walked out the front door and headed for the tractor mower. He didn't know how long the machine had been sitting out in the elements but was pleasantly surprised when it turned over on the second attempt.

As he mowed, his thoughts whirled in a million directions. The fact that two women who worked as waitresses at the café had been murdered bothered him, especially when he got a visual image of Courtney in the familiar black Cowboy Café T-shirt and jeans that all of the waitresses wore.

It wasn't his job to protect Courtney or any of the other women in the café. That job belonged to Sheriff Cameron Evans and his team of capable deputies. Nick just needed to mind his own business and let the sheriff do his job.

He was halfway through with the yard when Adam stepped out on the front porch, two cups of coffee in his hands. Nick shut down the tractor and joined his brother on the porch.

"Thanks," he said as he took the spare coffee from Adam. Even though he'd had his fill of coffee earlier, this felt like an olive branch of sorts from the brother he desperately wanted to connect with.

Together the two of them eased down in the wicker chairs on the porch, and for a moment neither of them spoke but merely sipped their coffee and stared out in the distance.

"I'll help chop up some of that brush after we finish our coffee," Adam said after a long, slightly uncomfortable silence. "Sorry I've let things go."

"I'd appreciate the help," Nick replied.

He finished his coffee, set the empty cup on the porch and then headed back to the tractor, wondering if his brother was really going to help or would disappear back into the house to find another bottle of booze to anesthetize his pain and escape reality with.

His heart filled with hope as Adam walked off the porch and headed toward the barn. He returned a moment later with a long-handled sickle to cut down the thick brush.

The brothers worked together until just after noon, then went inside to a lunch of ham and cheese sandwiches and ice-cold lemonade. This time the silence between them wasn't uncomfortable. It was merely the silence of two men who had worked hard and needed a few minutes to relax.

They worked throughout the afternoon and then at dinnertime showered up and headed for the café.

"You know Courtney Chambers?" Nick asked when they were in his truck.

"Sure, she's one of the waitresses at the café," Adam replied.

"Did you know she had a baby?" Nick's fingers tightened slightly around the steering wheel.

"Yeah, I remember somebody mentioning something about it at some point or another."

"You know how old the kid is?"

Nick felt Adam's gaze on him, but Nick kept his eyes carefully focused on the road. "I have no idea. Ten months or maybe a year or so. Why?"

"Just curious. She served me lunch yesterday when I showed up in town and I thought she was kind of cute."

"Off-limits, brother. She's from some hoity-toity family in Evanston and she's dating Grant Hubert, a banker. I'd lay odds that the kid is his and there's a wedding going to happen in the not-so-distant future."

Nick didn't even attempt to talk about the lump that suddenly appeared in his throat.

"If you plan on sticking around town for a while there are plenty of single, pretty women," Adam said.

"Then why haven't you found one?"

Adam gave him a dark glance. "You don't find many

available women in the bottom of a bottle of whiskey. I wouldn't mind a drink right now."

"Yeah, well, I would mind. Maybe it's time to pull your nose out of the bottle and take a look around," Nick said as he pulled into the café parking lot. "Looks busy."

"We're right in the middle of dinner rush," Adam replied. Together they got out of the truck and went into the establishment, where glasses clinked and conversation buzzed.

Nick spotted a booth being cleaned in Courtney's section. He quickly led Adam to that booth.

He saw the frown that danced across Courtney's face as they settled in. What was he doing? He felt as if he were picking at old wounds, tearing away scabs to make those wounds bleed. But he couldn't seem to stop himself.

Seeing her again had stirred up so many old emotions, feelings that he hadn't expected, didn't realize he possessed. He wasn't sure what to do with them, or how to resolve them with the present.

At the moment all he could do was place his dinner order with her. She was curt and professional as she took their orders, her gaze never quite meeting his.

As he walked away, Nick looked around the busy café, noticing people he'd never seen before. "Lots of unfamiliar faces," he said to Adam.

"Two years is a long time. People move away, new people move in."

"Who is the guy in the wheelchair?" Nick nodded toward a nearby table where a man in a motorized scooter sat at a table alone.

"Brandon Williams. He came to town about six months ago. Nice guy...war veteran. Had his legs shot up with shrapnel and it left him with some facial scarring, but he buzzes all over town in that scooter."

For the next few minutes Adam told Nick who some of the other unfamiliar people in the café were, and by that time Courtney arrived to bring their drink orders. As she set them down, Nick caught a whiff of her perfume beneath the scent of the cooking food. Jasmine. He'd asked her once what it was because he loved the smell of it on her skin.

She whirled away from the table and he felt the chill that emanated from her. He knew he'd hurt her when he'd left, but she'd obviously moved on pretty quickly. So, why was she holding such a grudge against him now?

And why on earth did he care? He had no intention of sticking around town. She apparently was happy with Mr. Banker Grant Hubert. It was over…long done. She was the past, and Nick tried to live his life never looking back.

Courtney felt as if she'd suddenly grown ten awkward thumbs and wooden legs that barely functioned, and it was all because he was here.

Why couldn't he eat at home or at least sit someplace where she didn't have to serve him, didn't even have to look at him? Why did he seem to be under her nose every time she turned around?

She wasn't even supposed to be here tonight, but Mary had called earlier in the day and told her she'd had two waitresses who had called in sick and asked if Courtney could work the dinner rush between five and seven.

Reluctantly she'd agreed because she could always use the extra money. But if she'd known that Nick would be here tonight, she would have just stayed at home with Garrett and had Mary contact one of the other waitresses not working tonight.

As she hurried away from their table and toward Brandon Williams, she was aware of Nick's gaze following her.

She wanted to turn around and scream at him to stop it, that it wasn't right that his gaze still had the power to warm her from top to bottom.

Instead she continued in the direction of Brandon. When she reached him she offered him a friendly smile. "Hi, Mr. Williams. How are you this evening?"

It was difficult to discern Brandon's age as his head was as bald as a cue ball and he had no eyebrows. A scar ran down the side of his plump face and the blue of his eyes radiated warmth. "I'm doing well, Courtney. How is that little fella of yours?"

"He's great. Talking more and more every day and becoming a bit of a ham. Now, what can I get for you this evening?"

By the time she'd put in Brandon's order, Nick's and Adam's plates were ready for delivery. She steeled herself and approached their booth once again. "Two Saturday night specials," she said as she placed the plates down before each of them. "Is there anything else you need?"

"I could use a refill on my iced tea," Nick said.

She looked at his half-empty glass. "Of course, I'll be right back." Moments later she returned to the table, with his iced tea glass filled to near overflowing, and then went back to dealing with her other customers.

Nick and Adam lingered, ordering coffee and Mary's famous apple pie for dessert. Courtney served them once again and then tried to keep her gaze away from

Nick as she busied herself taking care of other people's dining needs.

She smiled at one of her favorite customers, Thomas Manning. Thomas had arrived in Grady Gulch about a year ago. He was in his late thirties, quiet and well spoken and usually had a book in his hand. She took Thomas's order and left the table.

She couldn't wait for this rush hour to be over so she could get Garrett back home and get on with the rest of her weekend. All she wanted to do for the remainder of the evening and all day tomorrow was spend time with her favorite little boy.

Still, she couldn't help but notice several people stopping by the booth to visit with Nick and Adam. On their best day the two were both charmers, easy to talk to and drawing people to them.

The dinner rush seemed to last forever, but finally people began to filter out. She glanced over at Nick and saw that Mary was visiting with the two men.

As the pretty blonde walked away from their table to visit with another dinner guest, Nick's gaze caught hers and in the depths of his eyes was a burning anger.

He knows.

The words thundered in her head, for a moment stealing all other sound, as if she'd gone momentarily deaf. She broke eye contact with him and walked on shaky legs toward the kitchen.

He knows Garrett is his. She wasn't sure who might have told him Garrett's age, but with that information there would be little doubt in his mind that the boy belonged to him. She'd make him doubt, she thought desperately. As long as he didn't see Garrett, he couldn't be sure.

"Problems?" Rusty asked as he stepped away from

the grill. More than once Rusty had served as bouncer for customers who got out of line. He not only had broad shoulders and arms the size of tree trunks, but his face was enough to intimidate anyone.

He might scare somebody who didn't know him, but Courtney had seen the soft side he rarely displayed, his utter devotion to Mary and her son, Matt, and all the women who worked here.

"No problems," she quickly assured him as she tried to still the rapid rhythm of her heartbeat. "I just needed a minute away from the crowd."

What was she going to do? A frantic energy swelled up inside her as she considered her options. She could lie to him and tell him that a week after he'd left town she'd slept with somebody else. There would be no way he could disprove her words, and she wouldn't have to give him a specific name.

The only way he'd know the truth for sure was if he actually saw that little cleft in Garrett's chin. It couldn't have come from anyone else in the entire town but Nick Benson.

For the first time since she'd left her hometown of Evanston, she thought of going back. Would her parents have finally forgiven her for not being the daughter they'd wanted? Would they accept her and her child into their home to get back on her feet after having kicked her out when they'd discovered her pregnancy?

Surely two years would have brought some forgiveness. Even as she thought of the idea, she dismissed it. She hadn't heard from either of her parents since they'd thrown her out of their home. Even the birth of her son hadn't broken the deafening silence of disapproval that had lingered over the past fifteen months.

Besides, she couldn't go back to living beneath their

roof, where she'd always felt inadequate, where she'd never embraced their need for material things and social acceptance, and where they'd never accepted the woman she had grown up to be.

With a sigh she left the kitchen once again, noting with a quick, darting glance that Nick and Adam remained in their booth. She'd already given them their tab so there was nothing else they should need from her.

She focused on the remaining diners in her section and slowly began to relax as she once again met Nick's gaze and didn't see any of the fiery anger she thought she'd seen earlier.

Maybe she'd only imagined the flames of rage there. Maybe it had simply been her slightly guilty conscience at work. She picked up the glass of iced tea she'd nursed all through her shift from a small table close to the restrooms.

She took a sip of her tepid tea and for a moment she thought of the two waitresses who would never work here again, women who had been murdered in their beds.

Everyone had hoped that Candy's murder had either been committed by her boyfriend or perhaps a drifter passing through town. The latest murder seemed to blow the drifter theory out of the water. She set her glass down and fought against a shiver that threatened to walk up her spine as she realized the odds were good that the killer was a local. She might have even served him a meal.

She shook her head to dispel thoughts of murder and smoothed a hand down the T-shirt that marked her as a Cowboy Café waitress. Hopefully it was just a strange coincidence that both of the murder victims had worked here.

It was just before seven when Mary walked over to her. "You can go home now. Thanks for filling in at the last minute. This flu bug that's going around seems to be getting people down."

Courtney nodded, but she wondered if the two waitresses who had called in sick had really been sick or had been afraid to come in after the latest murder of one of their own.

She'd heard through the grapevine that Shirley's funeral was set for next Wednesday, and as far as Courtney knew everyone from the Cowboy Café planned to attend. Mary had already said she intended to close down the café for several hours that day.

"I'll see you Monday at noon," Courtney said as she handed Mary her order pan and pen. "Good night."

She'd almost made it to the door when a firm hand wrapped around her arm and stopped her. "We need to talk." Nick's voice simmered with barely controlled emotions just behind her.

She slowly turned to face him and realized she hadn't imagined that moment earlier when his eyes had flamed with anger. Now they were a cold, icy blue, and she knew if she didn't think fast on her feet, he'd know the secret she'd planned on taking to the grave.

Chapter 4

Nick held tight to her arm, not wanting to release her until he could bend her to his will, force her to tell him what he wanted to know.

"I told you before, we have nothing to talk about," she replied, her face taking on an unhealthy paleness.

"Oh, I think we do," he said, his voice deceptively soft and calm. "I think we have a lot to discuss."

She glanced around frantically and jerked her arm from his grasp. "I can't imagine what you're talking about. I'm tired. I just finished up a busy dinner shift. Leave me alone, Nick."

He watched as she stormed out the door, and he sensed his brother moving to stand just behind him. "Problems?" Adam asked.

"Maybe, maybe not," Nick said as the two left the café. "Drop me off at the motel."

"At the motel? Why? You want to tell me what's

going on?" Adam asked as Nick tossed him the keys to the truck.

"I think Courtney and I have a little unfinished business." Was it possible? Adam had told him he thought Courtney's baby was about ten months old, but Mary had mentioned she couldn't believe that Courtney's son was already fifteen months old. Was she mistaken?

Fifteen months? Was it possible the child was his? They'd always been so careful about birth control, except that last night when he'd come to her consumed with grief.

There had been no thought of birth control that night. There had been no thought in his mind except his need for Courtney's arms around him, his need for her to swallow him, to engulf him so as to somehow take away at least a little bit of his pain.

"Unfinished business? I didn't know you had any starting business with her," Adam said as he got in behind the wheel. He didn't start the engine but rather turned and looked at Nick in the passenger seat. "Again, you want to tell me what's going on? And this time, be a little more specific."

"At least start the engine so we can get some air-conditioning going," Nick replied. He drew a deep sigh and stared out the window, his brain whirling with suppositions. Was it possible she'd gotten pregnant that night?

If that was the case then why hadn't she called him? Why hadn't she let him know immediately? That was a question that had haunted him even before now.

In the time that he'd been gone he'd never changed his cell phone number, and even though he'd decided not to contact her, to let her go, he'd been surprised and more than a little hurt that she'd never attempted to call him.

Now there was a part of him that was infuriated that she hadn't called to tell him she was pregnant with his child. Slow down, he told himself. He couldn't be sure about the facts. He couldn't be sure that the child was his.

As the interior of the truck began to cool, Nick turned to look at his brother. "Before Cherry's death, Courtney and I were sort of seeing each other."

Adam frowned. "Sort of seeing each other? You mean like dating?"

Nick gave a curt nod of his head.

"Why didn't I know about it? I never heard anything about you and Courtney Chambers."

"That's the way we wanted it. We kept our relationship a secret. Her parents would have freaked out if they had known she was dating a no-count rancher like me." A small burn set off in the pit of his stomach. Had the truth been that she'd been ashamed of their relationship and had only used the disapproval of her parents as an excuse?

"So, what's the unfinished business?"

"Courtney's baby."

Adam raised a dark eyebrow. "What about the baby?"

"Didn't you hear Mary mention that Courtney's boy was fifteen months old?"

"Fifteen months…" Adam's voice trailed off as he did the mental math. "The kid is yours?"

"I can't be positive." Nick's gut churned. "But, I intend to find out. Just take me to the motel, and I'll find my own way home from there."

Adam left the café parking lot and shook his head

ruefully. "You and Courtney, it's hard to wrap my mind around it. You just don't seem like her type."

"I wasn't. We were just having fun together for a while." The words felt like a lie as they left Nick's lips. "We had no contact after I skipped town."

"What are you going to do if the boy is yours?" Adam asked.

A child.

A son.

"I'm not sure." Nick's head whirled at the thought of the child, but he couldn't find any real emotional purchase. He was numbed by the very idea. At the moment the thought of him having a son was merely a theory, and until that theory was proven he couldn't quite wrap his mind around it.

Adam pulled up in front of the motel. "It doesn't look like she's here."

Nick opened the passenger door to step out. "She'll be here." Sooner or later she had to come home, and he wasn't about to leave here without answers.

"You want to call me when you're finished here and I'll come back for you?" Adam asked. Nick frowned as he saw his brother lick his lips and look in the direction of The Corral.

"Adam, go home and I'll call you when it's time to pick me back up."

For a long moment Adam stared at him, then with a weary sigh of resignation, he nodded. "Okay, I'll go home and wait for you."

"I'll call you for a ride home," Nick agreed. Nick got out of the truck, and as he watched Adam drive away he admitted to himself that he had momentarily worried that Adam would leave here and drive directly to

The Corral for a few drinks. The last thing he wanted was to be responsible for Adam drinking and driving.

He moved to the side of the motel and stood beneath a stand of trees, half-hidden by the deepening shadows of the night.

If she saw him waiting for her she might just turn right around and drive away as quickly as she could.

He figured she'd gone to pick up the boy from wherever he went when she worked. The boy. He didn't even know his name. But, he still didn't know if he even had a right to know his name.

He'd known in some part of his grieving heart when he'd left here that he'd hurt her, but he'd thought it was best for both of them. She'd been ashamed of him. He'd convinced himself that she'd needed her parents' approval more than she'd ever needed him.

He'd been stunned when he'd realized he was her first lover. But, there was no reason to believe since that time that he'd been her only lover.

He tensed as he saw her car pull in and park in front of her unit. He didn't immediately approach her but instead remained where he was and watched as she got out of the car and then opened the back door to retrieve the baby.

She hurried inside as if afraid somebody might see her, as if somehow afraid that *he* would see her. He'd certainly seen enough to know that the baby wasn't some wee little thing she carried in one arm. He'd been a little chunk who had to be older than a year.

Timing was everything. He needed to know the timing of her pregnancy. And the time to find that out was right now. He didn't want to go another minute without knowing the truth.

Drawing a deep breath, still more than a little bit

numb at the possibility of what he might discover, he approached her door and knocked firmly.

A curtain shifted slightly and then dropped back in place at the window. "Go away," her voice said through the closed door.

"I'm here now, Courtney, and I'm not going away," he replied.

"I'll call Sheriff Evans," she replied.

"I have a feeling with two murders on his hands you'll have a hard time getting his attention."

His comment was met with silence, and for several long moments he thought she intended to ignore him. But he wasn't going to be ignored tonight.

Just as he was getting ready to knock on the door once again, she opened it and slid outside into the hot night air, pulling the door halfway closed as she had the last time he'd shown up here.

"I'm curious about your son," he said, cutting to the chase. He noted that her full, lush lips tightened into a thin slash of irritation. The flash of the nearby red neon sign advertising the Grady Gulch Motel cast a faint blush over her features.

"Why would you be curious about him?" Her entire body language was one of intense defensiveness, but her gaze met his boldly.

A tight pressure filled Nick's chest, a pressure that was both severe and painful. He knew what the pressure was…it was the question that begged to be answered, and he somehow knew that the answer might change his life forever.

"Is he mine?" He felt as if his heart stopped beating, as if by merely asking the question all the air in his lungs had been completely depleted.

She raised her chin. "Of course not. No," she added more firmly.

The air he thought was gone whooshed out of his lungs.

"Did you really think I just sat in my room night after night and cried my eyes out when you left here?" Her voice quivered slightly, and in that quiver Nick recognized that she was lying.

"There have been other men in my life since you left, Nick. In any case, it doesn't matter who Garrett's father is. It doesn't matter if he's somebody from Evanston or a cowboy who traveled through town. He's my son and I'm all he needs."

"I'd like to see him."

Her gaze darted away from his. "There's no reason for you to see him. Besides, he's sleeping."

"I can be quiet," Nick said persistently.

"I really don't want him disturbed." She tucked a strand of her shiny dark hair behind her ear, still not quite meeting his gaze.

"I plan on being in town for a while, Courtney. Why wouldn't you want me to see your son? Most mothers can't wait to show off their kids. Why do I get the feeling that you're intentionally trying to hide him from me?"

Suddenly he couldn't wait another minute. He had to know the truth, and the truth was she wasn't the kind of woman who would have fallen into bed with just anyone… With a lot of anyones from Evanston or some dusty cowboy riding through.

Without warning, he pushed past her and into the room. "Nick, stop!" she cried sharply. "You have no right."

The only light in the room was the one hanging over

a small table on the other side of the room from the crib, but it was enough illumination for Nick to see the little boy who pulled himself up to stand in the crib and eye Nick with a sleepy blue gaze and tousled dark curls.

Nick froze at the sight of the bright blue eyes, the colorful cowboy pajamas and the little cleft chin, so like the one that greeted him in his mirror each morning.

The entire world stopped. There was nothing else in the room, in the universe but him and the little boy he knew now with certainty was his son. He hadn't quite believed Mary. He hadn't really thought it possible. He had a son!

Garrett.

A joy he'd never imagined possible filled his very soul. Even though he and Courtney had talked about someday having a family, a boy first and then a girl, he'd never really seriously considered fatherhood.

And yet here it was in front of him, a drooling, grinning little boy who looked just like him. This changed everything. Any plans he had to return to Texas disappeared. He'd build a life here, a life his son could share with him.

He turned to look at Courtney, whose face was as pale as a ghost's and whose eyes were wide with anxiety. "Now we definitely need to talk," he said, a small knot of anger beginning to build in his chest.

She should have called him. Dammit, she should have told him that she was pregnant with his child. He would have come back, he would have been a part of it.

He'd missed so much already, not just the pregnancy and the birth itself, but also the first fifteen months of his child's life. He'd missed the first word, the first step...so many firsts that would never, could never be repeated.

He was determined not to miss anything else. He could see by the look on Courtney's face that she didn't want to talk, that she just wanted him to go away and stay away. But that wasn't about to happen.

"Tomorrow morning, around nine o'clock at the park," she finally said in resignation.

"And you'll bring my son with you." It wasn't a question but rather a statement of fact that brooked no argument.

She hesitated a long moment and then nodded.

It wasn't enough for him. He had a hundred questions for her, but the anger grew tighter in his chest and he knew now wasn't the time to ask his questions, to demand answers.

"I'll see you in the morning," he said.

She didn't reply as he stepped back out the door. Instead the door closed behind him and he heard the click of the lock being engaged.

He pulled his cell phone from his pocket and punched in Adam's cell number. He answered on the first ring. "Ready for me to come back for you?"

"Ready."

"I'll be right there."

Nick pocketed the phone and then moved toward the trees at the edge of the complex where he'd previously stood to await her return home.

A son.

He had a son.

The thought thrilled him but also inspired more than a little bit of terror inside him. What in the hell did he have to offer a child? The family ranch needed so much work, Adam was in a fragile state of mind and Sam was in jail awaiting trial on attempted murder charges.

Some family tree.

Hell, he couldn't exactly use his own upbringing to help him in how to be a parent. His own mother and father had been cold, distant people who seemed content with each other but didn't know how to connect with any of their children.

When Nick had been almost fifteen they'd planned a getaway trip to Kansas City for their anniversary, but on their way home had been involved with an accident with a speeding big rig that had left them both dead.

At twenty-two years old, Sam had petitioned the courts to be guardian of his three younger siblings and had managed to convince the powers that be that he was capable. So, the siblings had stayed together and finished raising themselves. And now he had a son to raise.

Garrett.

Nick still couldn't wrap his mind around it. Fatherhood was all too new to him; he didn't know exactly what happened next. What did he know about being a father?

All he knew for certain was that Courtney had been part of his past until he saw that little boy in the crib. Now, at least for the next eighteen years or so, he and Courtney were forever bound by the child who had been conceived in a barn stable amid a cloud of grief.

One thing was clear. There wasn't going to be a happy reunion between him and Courtney. Their time together had come and gone, they'd never been right for each other and he wasn't about to attempt a new relationship with her for Garrett's sake.

But, he needed to get the ranch in shape, make one of the rooms into a little boy's playroom. He needed to be the man that little boy needed in his life. One way or another he intended to be an integral part of Garrett's life, with or without Courtney's approval.

* * *

Courtney awoke just after one in the morning, her heart racing as if trying to jump out of her chest. The room was in total darkness and she heard nothing unusual, but an icy chill stole over her, a cold that felt like her body's response to a nearby threat.

For the hundredth time she cursed the fact that she hadn't yet bought a small lamp to go on the nightstand next to her bed. What had wakened her? What caused her breath to catch with barely suppressed panic?

She could hear the faint sounds of Garrett's sleep breaths, normal and slightly calming. Sitting up, she once again looked around, trying to pierce the darkness of the room in an effort to find a reason for her edge of panic.

At that moment, against the faint red light that radiated through the thin curtains at the window, she saw a shadow pass by. Once again her heart banged painfully hard against her ribs.

Had somebody been standing there outside her window? Attempting to peer inside? She jumped out of the bed, silently cursing when she stubbed her big toe on the foot of Garrett's crib as she hurried to the motel room door. She checked to make sure the lock was in place and then went to the window and with trembling fingers pulled the curtain aside.

The parking lot was bathed in the cherry light from the motel sign. Cars were parked neatly before the units their owners had rented for the night, but she saw no one who could have made the shadow she'd seen.

Was somebody there hiding behind a car? Had somebody tried to open her door, and was that what had awakened her from her sleep? Was it the person who had killed two waitresses now stalking his next victim?

Or had it simply been somebody walking from a room to the vending area nearby? Her heart began to slow to a more normal pace.

She was definitely jumping at shadows. She flipped the switch that turned on the light over the table. It was probably her encounter with Nick that had her so distressed. A sharp icicle of panic still stabbed the back of her throat.

A cup of tea. That's what she needed at the moment. Her mother had always made a big production of teatime. She'd be appalled if she saw Courtney now pull out the battered old teakettle from the lower of the small set of cabinets, and the chipped cup from the upper cabinet.

No Earl Grey here, just the cheapest generic brand she could find. She put the kettle of water on to boil and then placed a tea bag in her cup, wishing that by drinking a single cup of tea she could banish Nick Benson from her mind, from her life, forever.

It had probably been dreams of him that had pulled her from her sleep, panicked and feeling threatened, not some nebulous shadow of somebody walking by her room.

She'd been a fool to think she could keep Garrett a secret from him. The minute Nick had shown up back in town she had been doomed. She'd just felt as if she were getting her life back on course, dating Grant and keeping up with the financial strain of single parenting on a waitress's salary.

She felt as if she'd been on track for building a future for herself and her son, and now Nick was like a wrench thrown in to screw things up.

The teakettle began a soft whistle and she quickly moved it off the burner and poured the steaming water into the awaiting cup. Once the tea was made, she sank down at the tiny table and drew a deep breath to steady her tumultuous emotions.

Part of the problem was she'd never really resolved her feelings about Nick. For months after he'd left, she'd hated him as she'd never hated another person in her life. She'd felt both bewildered and betrayed by his sudden absence.

What did he want from her now? What did he want of Garrett? Her biggest concern was that for Nick, Garrett would be a fun novelty for a couple of months, just as she had been in Nick's life, and then he'd disappear once again.

She'd rather have no father or a good stepfather than a father who drifted in and out of his life without responsibility, without any thought of long-term consequences to the child.

She certainly didn't want any kind of a personal relationship with him. Fool me once, shame on you. Fool me twice, shame on me, she thought as she finished her tea and put the cup in the sink.

She walked back to the motel room door and once again checked to make sure the lock was securely fastened. There was no question that every woman in town was more than a little bit jumpy over the two unsolved murders.

She turned off the light and made her way through the darkness back into bed, even though she knew sleep would probably remain a distant pleasure for hours to come.

The next thing she knew, the morning sun was peeking through the slit in the curtains, and a glance at her clock let her know it was just after seven.

Garrett was still sleeping, but she knew it wouldn't

be long and he'd be up and ready for his breakfast. She had so much to do in order to meet Nick at the park at nine.

As she took a quick shower and tried not to anticipate what might come of the meeting, she reminded herself that at least for the moment she was the one in control. He wasn't even listed on the birth certificate as the father. That particular box had been marked unknown.

By eight forty-five she had herself and Garrett dressed and fed and him loaded into his car seat in her car. "Bye-bye," Garrett said as she started the car engine.

"That's right," she said. "We're going bye-bye."

Her heart thrummed an unsettled rhythm as she headed in the direction of the city park. As she drove down Main Street she saw Cameron Evans and a couple of his deputies walking along the sidewalk and knew they were probably interviewing and investigating the murder of Shirley Cook.

There was no question that it was more than a little disturbing that there had been two waitresses murdered in the past three months and neither crime had been solved.

She thought of that moment in the middle of the night when she'd awakened panicked and thought that somebody was outside her motel room door. She knew somebody had been out there, but she couldn't know if it had simply been an innocent presence or something more sinister.

But, at the moment she had other things to worry about…like Nick and Garrett. She didn't even like thinking of the two of them in the same sentence.

As she pulled into the parking lot of the small park that boasted swings and a slide and a sandbox that Garrett loved, Nick's truck was already there. She steeled herself as she parked next to his truck, as afraid now as she had been in the middle of the night when she'd imagined the possibility that a killer was stalking her.

Chapter 5

As he stepped out of the driver's door, his dark cowboy hat pulled down low over his brow, Courtney was shocked by a sudden visceral attraction that pierced through her. It was the same reaction she'd had when she'd first seen him coming out of the feed store in Evanston.

At that time she'd felt as if a rocket had gone off in the pit of her stomach, and he'd later told her he'd felt that same way when he'd first laid eyes on her.

He walked toward her car with that loose-hipped gait that made him appear to be a carefree cowboy, but when he tipped his hat back and she saw his eyes, there was nothing carefree in those blue depths.

"Good morning," he said, his gaze on Garrett still in the car seat. Nick looked slightly nervous, shifting his weight from one foot to the other.

"Out!" Garrett demanded and clapped his hands with

excitement. He knew the park. Courtney brought her son here often.

"Mind if I get him out?" Nick asked tentatively.

She wanted to tell him no, that she didn't want him touching her son, but she knew that wasn't right, that it wouldn't be fair.

"Go ahead," she agreed around the huge lump in her throat.

She stepped back and watched as he carefully unfastened Garrett while he pulled off Nick's hat and laughed with glee.

As Nick gathered the child into his arms and straightened, Courtney saw the look in Nick's eyes, the expression that swept over his sinfully handsome features.

She knew that look. She knew exactly what he was feeling at that moment. It was the same thing she'd felt after she'd given birth and they'd placed Garrett into her arms for the very first time.

Awe.

It was an awe that sucked the very breath out of you, weakened your bones and humbled you in a way that nothing else would ever do again.

The moment was broken as Garrett grabbed Nick's nose. "Nose," he said proudly.

Nick laughed, and the sound of it attempted to wrap around Courtney's heart, but she steeled herself against it. She'd always loved the sound of his laughter. "Yes, that's my nose and you're pulling it off," Nick said as he pulled Garrett's fingers away.

Courtney leaned into the car and retrieved Nick's hat, a diaper bag and a small tote that carried toys for the sandbox. She motioned Nick in that direction as she passed him his hat.

Next to the big box of fine white sand was a picnic

table and beyond that a thick stand of trees. They could sit at the table and talk while Garrett played.

As they walked, Nick continued to look at his son, as if matching features with his own, as if still processing the fact that Garrett was a reality now in his arms.

They didn't speak to each other until Garrett was situated in the sandbox with several plastic trucks, a shovel and a pail. Courtney sat on one side of the picnic table and Nick sat on the other, facing her.

The anger she'd seen the night before in his eyes was gone, replaced by a quiet simmer of an emotion she couldn't quite identify. Her heart hammered the uneven rhythm of anxiety. She just didn't know what to expect from him.

"Why didn't you tell me when you first found out you were pregnant?" he finally asked. "You had my cell phone number. I never changed it."

An edge of bitterness washed over her. "By the time I realized I was pregnant, two and a half months had gone by since you'd left town. I never changed my phone number and yet you never called me either."

She tried desperately to keep the pain, that touch of bitterness, out of her voice and instead simply make it a statement of fact. "I figured if you had any interest at all in me, in what was going on with my life, then I would have heard from you."

Nick took off his hat and set it on the table next to him, his gaze on Garrett, who was happily filling his pail with the white sand. "You still should have called me," he repeated. "This was bigger than both of us. I had a right to know."

"You gave up all your rights when you left me without a word." They were going around and around on the same topic, one that couldn't be changed. "I was a little too busy planning my own future to worry about you," she replied tersely.

He gazed at her curiously. "And how is it that your future became waitressing in Grady Gulch?"

A wealth of emotion pressed tight in her chest as she thought of those days and weeks right after she'd discovered she was pregnant with Nick's baby.

For weeks she'd kept the secret, terrified and so alone. But, by the time she was almost four months pregnant she knew she had to tell her parents, although they would be disappointed in her.

She'd lived her life trying to be the daughter they wanted, the daughter they'd tried to mold into something great, and until she'd met Nick she'd done and been everything they'd asked of her.

They hadn't considered college necessary because their intention was for her to be the arm candy of a wealthy, influential man. So instead of college, she'd had tennis lessons and spent time with her mother in New York. She'd been trained in ballroom dancing and taught all the social skills that would make her a great wife for a great man.

"Needless to say my parents weren't thrilled when they found out I was pregnant," she finally said. The scene the night that she'd confessed to them was forever burned into her memory. She knew she'd let them down, but she'd also believed they loved her enough to support her in her time of need.

"They demanded to know who the father was, and when I refused to tell them they kicked me out of the house and disowned me." A lump rose in her throat, but she consciously swallowed against it. Nick had betrayed her first, and then her parents had followed suit.

A tiny frown line appeared across his forehead as

she continued. "So, I packed up my bags, called a friend to pick me up and went to Mary and the Cowboy Café. You'd spoken so highly of her and I knew she had a reputation for taking in people in crisis and letting them work and live in one of the little cottages behind the restaurant." She shrugged. "And that's how I happen to be here."

Of course it hadn't been that easy. She'd been terrified and alone. She'd been afraid she couldn't make it, that somehow she couldn't be a single mother. Yet, despite her fears, the moment she'd discovered her pregnancy she'd also realized a tremendous love for the baby she carried. She knew that somehow she'd find the strength to make it work.

He didn't say anything for a long moment. "Are things better with your parents now?"

"I haven't seen or spoken to them since the night they threw me out. But, I'm fine and I've learned not to depend on anyone but myself. So, what do you want, Nick?"

Her heart, which had already begun to beat too fast, stepped up in rhythm, aching in her chest as she stared at the man she had once believed she knew better than anyone else. She realized now she hadn't known him at all, and after two years she definitely didn't know the man who sat across from her.

"I want joint custody." His gaze met hers boldly, shining with determination.

For a moment the wind was knocked out of her. She'd thought he'd probably want some sort of informal visitation while he was in town, but she'd never expected for him to ask for this.

"Why?" she asked flatly.

The frown in his forehead deepened. "Why? Because he's my son. Because I want to be a part of his life."

"For how long?

"What do you mean for how long? For the rest of my life," he replied with a touch of irritation.

"Or as long as something bad doesn't happen and you decide to run again. Or until it all gets too complicated and you can't handle it anymore." She shook her head. "I'll be glad to work with you on some kind of visitation schedule, but joint custody is out of the question."

The muscles in his jaw tightened and his eyes narrowed. "I can do this with you or without you, Courtney. Don't fight me on this."

It was her nightmare come true. She didn't want to officially invite Nick into her son's life, but she also knew he could accomplish what he wanted. He could tie her up in a court battle, a battle she couldn't afford to wage. He could force a paternity suit and make a case for joint custody. She raised a shaky hand to tuck a strand of her hair behind her ear, searching for a way out of this untenable situation.

"Nick, this has all hit me like a ton of bricks," she said truthfully. Almost as bad as him wanting custody was the fact that on some physical level he still affected her.

He wore the same woodsy cologne he'd worn when they had been lovers, and it still created an unexpected warmth inside her as she remembered being held in his arms. "Can we just take everything slow for a couple of weeks and see how it goes?" she asked.

He hesitated a moment and then slowly nodded. "You know, I could babysit him when you're working at the café."

"You wouldn't even know how to change a diaper," she exclaimed.

He grinned, the slow lazy smile that had once melted her heart. "At least I know what end to diaper. I'm sure I could figure out the rest of it when duty called."

She shook her head and looked at Garrett, who was now pouring sand over his own head. "I don't want to disrupt his schedule all of a sudden. Sophie Martinez has been watching him while I work since he was born. Like I said, we need to take this slow not just for my sake, but for his sake, as well."

Nick got up and walked over to Garrett, and for a moment Courtney feared he intended to snatch the boy away and run to his truck. Instead he leaned down and gently swept the sand from Garrett's short, dark, curly hair and handed him the little blue shovel.

Garrett gave him a smile that would melt anyone's heart. Courtney wished at that moment Garrett was throwing a temper fit, or filling his diaper with a particularly nasty poo, doing something…anything that might make Nick rethink his plans.

"We'll do it your way for now and take things slow for a couple of weeks," Nick finally said as he returned to the picnic table. "But, I'd like for you to arrange so that I can spend a little time with him each day. He needs to get to know me, and I want to get to know him."

"I'm sure I can arrange that," she replied, thinking of how complicated everything was going to be from now on.

"How about we start with all of us having dinner together tonight," he said.

"I already have plans for dinner," she replied. Grant

had called her right before she'd left the motel that morning and asked her and Garrett out for dinner.

Besides, she didn't want to make the visitations with Garrett about herself and Nick. Dinner felt far too intimate and would only lead to even more complications that she didn't want or need.

His gaze narrowed, as if he was unhappy with whatever plans she'd made for the evening. Tough, she thought. He wasn't about to waltz back into town and insinuate himself into her life again. This was about him and Garrett and nothing else.

"I work from noon to eight during the next week," she said. "Why don't I plan on meeting you here every morning around ten? You can spend an hour or so with him before I take him to Sophie's." She could tell her compromise didn't sit well with him. "At least it will give Garrett a chance to get accustomed to being around you."

"Okay," he finally agreed. "We'll do that for a week and then see what happens after that."

She didn't want to see what happened next. She just wished she could will him far away from Grady Gulch and the son who was her very heart and soul.

He got up from the picnic table and grabbed his hat. "I'm not going to run away again when things get tough," he said as he placed the hat back on his head. "I'm here to stay, Courtney, and you're going to have to just deal with it. You're going to have to deal with me."

He leaned down and chucked Garrett beneath his chin, then dodged as Garrett attempted to grab his hat. "I'll see you tomorrow, little guy."

Courtney watched as he walked back to his truck, her emotions in turmoil. Despite everything that had happened between them, Nick Benson still stirred inside her a yearning, a longing, a desire that she didn't feel and would probably never feel for Grant.

It wasn't until the truck disappeared from the parking lot that she managed to draw a full, cleansing breath. She still didn't believe him. She was convinced he'd hang around for only a couple of weeks, maybe a month at the most, and then he'd go back to Texas, where she'd heard he'd been happy.

Here he would be faced daily with the prospect of being a single father, the fact that Adam was quickly becoming an alcoholic and the everyday reminder that his eldest brother was a criminal.

He'd run before. She was confident he'd run again. It was just a matter of time. Only this time when he ran, he wouldn't be taking her heart with him.

She let Garrett play for another half an hour in the sandbox and then with the sun starting to get hot, she loaded up the toys, slung both the tote and the diaper bag over her elbow and helped Garrett to his feet.

"Bye-bye?" he asked as he grabbed firmly to her hand.

"Yes, we're going bye-bye. We're going home and you're taking a nice bath."

He let out a string of words that Courtney didn't understand, but she smiled. "That's right," she agreed. Whatever he'd said, her answer must have been correct for he returned her smile and they began to slowly make their way back toward her car.

They were halfway there when she felt it, a sharp prickling in the center of her back, a sense that she and Garrett weren't alone in the park. But the parking lot was empty other than her car, and she'd seen no other children or adults anywhere in the area.

Still, the uneasiness she felt nearly overwhelmed her,

made her feel half-sick to her stomach. Whether it was instinct or paranoia, the strong feeling raised the hairs on the nape of her neck.

She turned her head and glanced behind them. The picnic table was empty, and there was nobody in sight. Her gaze shifted to the thick stand of trees.

Was somebody there? Watching her? Watching them? Was it the same somebody who had been outside her motel room last night?

She stopped walking despite Garrett pulling impatiently on her hand. She stared at the trees, seeking a source of the bad feeling that crashed through her, yet seeing nothing.

As crazy as it seemed, she felt a presence there, a malevolent energy emanating from the thick wooded area in the near distance.

As if tuning in to the same thing, Garrett began to cry. With sudden panic, Courtney picked him up in her arms, held him tight against her chest and ran toward her car, her heart pounding with an inexplicable fear.

She didn't feel safe until they were locked in the car and headed back to her motel, and even then the sense of safety was fragile.

The knowledge that somebody had killed two waitresses who worked at the Cowboy Café was never far from her mind. Had the killer been in the woods watching them? Watching her?

Was it really possible that she'd been targeted as the next victim?

Chapter 6

Before heading back to the ranch, Nick decided to stop at the Cowboy Café for an early lunch. His intention had been to stay longer at the park, to play with Garrett, but after hashing things through with Courtney he'd felt the need to get some distance from her, to think and absorb and plan what happened next.

He wasn't sure what exactly would happen next, but despite Courtney's doubts, despite her desire to the contrary, he was in this for the long run.

He walked into the café, hung his hat on the wall and then took a stool at the counter next to Sheriff Cameron Evans, who looked like a dead man walking as he picked listlessly at the handful of French fries left on his plate.

"Hey, Sheriff." Nick greeted the handsome man, who looked as if a bone-weary exhaustion had claimed every ounce of his energy.

"Nick, good to see you again," Cameron replied with a faint smile. "I'd heard through the grapevine that you were back in town."

Nick was grateful he didn't mention the family issues that had ultimately brought Nick home. None of it needed to be said. "I can tell by looking at you that your investigation into the murders isn't going so well."

Cameron frowned. "I feel like I'm chasing a damned ghost. Twice he's managed to get into women's places of residence and kill them without leaving behind a single hair, a fiber or a witness. We're all still trying to sniff out a trail to follow, but so far there's none."

"You think the other waitresses who are working here are in some kind of danger?" Nick asked, thinking of Courtney.

A deep sigh released from Cameron. "To be honest, I don't know what to think anymore. However, I have warned everyone who works here to make sure their doors and windows are locked tight when they are at home. In Candy's case, the door on the cabin was either unlocked or she invited the killer into her place. In Shirley's case, the killer apparently entered through an open window in her living room. Easy access." He shook his head.

Nick digested this information as he thought about the motel room that Courtney was currently calling home. There was only one door in the unit and the front windows, and he assumed there was probably a window in the bathroom.

But surely living in a motel where there were people staying on each side of her unit, where there was some kind of traffic at any given time, would keep her safe. A killer would be foolish to pick a place where people came and went at all hours of the day and night.

At that moment Mary stepped up behind the counter in front of the two men. "Hi, Nick. How are things going?"

"I'm a dad." He blurted out the words before he had time to think.

He wasn't sure who looked more shocked, the sheriff or Mary. "Then I guess congratulations are in order," Mary said. "Did this happen while you were down in Texas?"

"No, actually it happened before I left for Texas. Garrett is my son."

Once again, stunned surprise crossed Mary's pretty features. "Courtney's Garrett? He's your son?"

Nick nodded, a lump rising in his throat as the full impact of fatherhood hit him square in the chest. From now on each and every action he took, every decision he made would reflect on him not just as a man, but also as a father.

"Well, what a surprise," Mary exclaimed.

"Yeah, it was kind of a major surprise for me, too."

"Now that you mention it, I see the resemblance between you and the boy," Cameron replied as he slid off his stool. "He's definitely got your chin. And now I've got to get back to work."

He nodded to Nick and then gave a gentle smile to Mary. "I'll be in touch."

Mary returned the smile, a light in her eyes that made Nick wonder if there wasn't something brewing between the two of them.

When Cameron had left the café, Mary turned her attention back to Nick. "So, what do you plan to do about all this?"

"My original plan when I got into town was to try to

straighten out things with Adam and the ranch and then return to Texas as soon as possible," he said.

"And now?"

"And now, of course everything has changed," he replied, once again a feeling of awe swelling in his chest as he thought of Garrett. "I'm here to stay and be a father to that little boy. In fact, I just met with Courtney at the park to set up some kind of initial visits with Garrett. Eventually I want joint custody."

"Is there any chance of you and Courtney making a go of it again?" Mary asked, displaying her penchant for matchmaking.

"None," Nick replied flatly. "We've both moved on from where we were before I left Grady Gulch two years ago. It's all about Garrett now. We just have to figure out a way to work together in parenting him, but other than that there's nothing between us and never will be again."

"At least it's nice that you intend to step up. So many men don't, and every little boy needs his daddy in his life. Now, what can I get you to eat?"

Nick placed his order and waved at Junior Lempke, who gave him a shy smile and ducked his head as he peeked out of the kitchen.

Every little boy needs his daddy in his life. Mary's words resonated deep inside him. Even though there had been a father in Nick's life, he'd never had a daddy. Tom Benson had been a quiet man who worked the ranch during the day and ignored his family in the evenings.

Even Nick's mother had been a distant figure, fawning over the man of the house at the expense of her children. Cherry had been the mother figure in Nick's life, and for all intents and purposes there had been no father.

Nick intended to be the father his own had never

been. He wanted to be present and available any time of day or night for Garrett. He was determined to be the best father any boy could ever have.

The tinkle of the bell over the front door turned Nick in his stool. He stiffened as he saw Daniel Jefferson and a woman he assumed was Lizzy Wiles come through the door. They went to a booth by the window as Nick turned back around.

Lizzy Wiles. The woman Nick's brother had tried to kill. Since the moment Nick had heard about Sam's crime, he'd tried not to think about it, not to process it.

Sam had always been the strong one in the family, taking care of the ranch business and making sure his younger siblings were all right.

Even though he hadn't been particularly close to his eldest brother, he'd depended on him to be the rock in the family, the glue that held them all together after their parents' unexpected death.

For the first time since he'd heard of his brother's incarceration, he felt a little of what Adam must be feeling... A sense of intense betrayal and a deeper sense of shame.

He turned around once again and met Daniel's gaze, relief washing over him as Daniel gave him a friendly nod. That was all it took to move Nick off his stool and toward the booth.

There had been a time when Daniel and all of the Benson brothers had been good friends. They lived on neighboring ranches and had all grown up together.

"Hi, Nick. Nice to see you back in town," Daniel said. There was no trace of tension in his tone.

"Thanks, it's good to be back." Nick turned his gaze to the woman with the light brown hair and amber eyes.

"And you must be Lizzy." She nodded and Nick continued, "I just want to say…"

She held up a hand to stop him midsentence. "Not necessary," she replied, as if knowing he'd intended to deliver an apology. "We've all suffered since Daniel's wife's and your sister's deaths. I don't have any issues with you. It's nice to meet you, Nick." She offered him a bright smile that somehow managed to assuage any guilt he might feel.

"I just wanted to come over and say hello," he said, now feeling slightly awkward.

"Hello back," she replied, a humorous twinkle in her eye. "We're good, Nick. The past is done and I'm over it."

Daniel gazed at Lizzy with a lazy amusement coupled with an obvious love, and as Nick moved back to his seat he remembered the time that he'd felt not just wild, crazy passion for Courtney, but also a deep, abiding love.

Initially when they'd begun to date, he'd found the idea of seeing her in secret exciting and fun. He'd call or text her and they'd rendezvous in the old barn, where they'd spend hours talking with the faint scent of hay and horse surrounding them. But after a couple of months, the novelty had worn off and he began to press her for a more public relationship.

She'd balked, terrified of what her parents would think if they found out she was dating a cowboy. Nick had been surprised at the amount of power her parents still held in her life. But since he'd been without parents for so long, he'd given her the benefit of the doubt.

Still, in the weeks just before Cherry's death, he'd pressed her even harder to meet her parents, to go to dinner together, to be seen together as a couple. He was unable to see how he and Courtney could possibly have a future together if they couldn't even be seen in public.

Then Cherry's death had happened, and Nick's world had been turned upside down. On the day of her funeral, Nick had sunk into the darkest place he'd ever known. The sister he'd adored was gone, and in that dark place he recognized that there was no future for him with a woman who was too afraid to be seen in public with him even in his greatest time of need.

When the funeral was over, Nick had packed his bags and left town, certain that in the long run he was doing what was best for both him and for Courtney. She could find a man she wasn't ashamed of, a man she could take home to meet her parents.

Funny, he'd gotten out of her life so she could continue to maintain being the daughter her parents needed her to be, but ultimately he'd been the reason that she'd been kicked to the curb.

He couldn't imagine what she'd gone through, and there was a part of his heart that ached because he hadn't been here to support her, to take care of her. She'd gone through the abandonment from her parents all alone. She'd gone through her pregnancy and the birth process equally alone.

Or maybe Grant had been there for her, holding her hand as she pushed to give birth to Nick's son. This thought made him slightly sick to his stomach. While he wouldn't have wanted her to be alone, he wished he would have been the man who'd been there for her.

As Mary placed his burger in front of him, he shoved away thoughts of the past. What was important was that he was here now, and even though he knew his and Courtney's time had passed, he intended to be a father to the son he already loved.

* * *

The afternoon passed quickly for Courtney. She gave Garrett a long bath. He was like a fish in the tub, splashing and playing with boats and toy frogs. He always fussed when she finally managed to pull him out of the water. By that time he was ready for his nap.

As Garrett napped, Courtney took her shower and picked out her clothes to wear to dinner that night, then, clad in a light-weight, short bathrobe, she sat at the table with a cup of tea and tried to process the emotions that roiled inside her head.

Nick still made her feel things that no other man had ever made her feel. One look from his brilliant blue eyes and her heart fluttered uncontrollably in her chest, her body heat rose more than just a little bit and she not only thought of their love-making, but also their laughter and the feeling of belonging she'd always had with him.

She didn't want him back. She would never be able to trust him again, would never be able to swallow the bitterness and sense of betrayal he'd left behind, the resentment that still lingered inside her.

But the old feelings he'd stirred inside her made her realize she'd rather be alone than accept the tepid relationship she had going with Grant.

If she looked deep within her soul, she knew what she felt for Grant was a warm friendship, but the thought of being intimate with him actually made her feel a little bit ill.

She knew Grant was expecting their relationship to eventually advance to an intimate level, and she also knew that to keep seeing him would be unfair. She didn't want to marry Grant. She wasn't sure she'd ever be ready to marry anyone.

As she finished her cup of tea, she knew that tonight

she had to finish her budding relationship with Grant. He was a nice man and someday he would meet a nice woman who would make him an equally nice wife, but that woman wasn't going to be Courtney.

It was just after six when Grant arrived to pick them up. The plans were to drive to Rockville, a nearby town where they had a pizza place that catered to children.

Initially she'd thought to have the breakup discussion with Grant before they even left her motel room, but he was so excited about taking Garrett to the restaurant, she didn't have the heart to do it then.

The ride to Rockville was a little over twenty minutes and Garrett kept them entertained, jabbering like a magpie from his car seat in the back.

Grant was good at meaningless conversation. He spoke about the weather and the upcoming town festival, uncontroversial chitchat that would have set her at ease if she didn't know that before the night was over she intended to tell him she wasn't going to see him again.

By the time they arrived at Kids' Pizza Palace, Courtney's stomach was in a bundle of knots as she tried to think of the best time, the best words to choose to let Grant know she didn't intend to date him anymore. She didn't want to hurt him, but if she was going to she'd rather do it now than a week or a month from now.

As Grant carried Garrett into the establishment, Garrett's eyes were huge as they were greeted by the flashing lights of games and colorful characters walking around in costume. The noise level was definitely not conducive to conversation.

As they seated themselves at a booth, with Garrett in a high chair at the end, a waitress hurried over to greet them. "Welcome to Kids'. Can I start you off with something to drink?"

It was difficult to hear her over the raucous noise of arcade games and squealing children, but they managed to place their order for both their drinks and a supreme pizza. Courtney ordered mac and cheese off the kids menu for Garrett and figured she could feed him some of the toppings off the pizza, as well.

The dinner was interminable for Courtney, whose head began to ache within five minutes of being seated. With conversation nearly impossible, she found herself looking around and noting the families that were enjoying the place.

Fathers and sons played video games together, and mothers stood by cheering each of them. A family of six sat at a large table nearby, their laughter drifting to Courtney's ears.

She tried to imagine herself here in a year from now...two years from now. Garrett would be old enough to enjoy some of the playground equipment, perhaps play some of the more elementary games. No matter how hard she tried, she couldn't place Grant in that picture, and she certainly couldn't place Nick there.

By the time they'd finished eating, her head banged with a nauseating intensity, and she didn't know if the headache was from the noise, the food or the fact that once they got back to her place she was going to tell a nice, respectable man that she didn't want to date him anymore.

It took only ten minutes in the car heading home for Garrett to fall asleep.

"I guess maybe Kids' was kind of a bad idea," Grant said, breaking the silence that had filled the car.

Courtney smiled at him. "Garrett is still a little young for that kind of thing, but I appreciate the thought."

"When a friend told me about it he didn't mention that the noise level made it impossible to talk and the pizza was substandard."

"Really, it's okay," Courtney assured him. "Garrett loved the mac and cheese, and the pizza was just fine and it was fun to watch all the other children and their parents enjoying the games."

"Next time I'll plan a quiet dinner for the three of us, with good food and a better ambiance for talking," he replied.

Do it now, a little voice whispered in her head. *Tell him now before he plans any other dates, before he says anything else about future plans.*

"Grant, I need to talk about us," she began, fumbling for the right words.

He flashed her a quick smile and then returned his attention to the road ahead. "What about us?"

"You're a wonderful man, Grant," she began.

There was a moment of silence. "Uh-oh, that doesn't sound good," he said, his voice deep and somber. "Especially if you intend to follow that sentence up with the fact that someday I'll make somebody a wonderful husband, but it's not going to be with you."

She drew a deep breath. "That's exactly what I was going to say next."

He was silent for several long moments. "Does this have something to do with Nick Benson being back in town?"

She looked at him in surprise. Surely he didn't know that Nick was Garrett's father. Nick had found out himself only the night before. "Why would you ask that?"

He shot her another smile, this one tinged with sadness. "You know how the rumor mill works around this town. I heard that you and Garrett and Nick spent some time together this morning at the park."

"We did," she admitted. "And I'm sure it won't be long before you hear that Nick is Garrett's father, but that has nothing to do with you and me and the decision I've come to about us."

He flashed her a quick glance. "Are you and Nick getting back together?" His voice held a harsh edge that she'd never heard before.

"Absolutely not," she said firmly. "Although there's no question we're going to have to work out some details where Garrett is concerned."

By this time they had reached her motel. He pulled up and parked the car, but neither of them made a move to get out. "Have I done something wrong?" he asked.

She hated the hurt and the faint anger she heard in his voice and the fact that she had put it there. "No, not at all." She released a deep sigh. "The problem isn't you, Grant. It's me. I care about you, but not in a romantic way. It isn't fair for me to continue to see you knowing that I don't have the kinds of feelings for you that would lead to a real relationship."

He dropped his hands from the steering wheel and held her gaze. "Are you sure those romantic feelings won't eventually grow with time? Because, I have to tell you, Courtney, what I feel for you is definitely romantic in nature. It's been all I could do to restrain myself from wrapping you in my arms, from kissing you until you're breathless whenever I spend time with you."

Courtney managed to staunch the shudder his words attempted to evoke, and it was at that moment she absolutely knew she was making the right decision.

"I'm sorry, Grant. I wish I felt the same way about you, but I just don't," she said softly.

He released a deep sigh. "I guess you can't force it if it isn't there. Then I guess we'll call it a night and we'll see each other around town."

He got out of the car, always the gentleman, and opened the back door to get the sleeping Garrett out of his car seat. As he carried Garrett to the door, Courtney fumbled in her purse for her key.

She felt awful, but she knew she'd done the right thing. She unlocked the door and flipped on the light as Grant carried Garrett into the room and set him gently on the bed, then turned to Courtney.

"I wish you happiness, Courtney. I'd hoped you could find it with me," he said as he walked back toward the door.

"I'd like it if we could remain friends."

His brown eyes were darker than usual. "I might need a little bit of time for that." With these words, he turned and went out the door.

With a deep sigh, Courtney closed and locked the door behind him. Alone. She hadn't felt this utterly alone since the night her parents had kicked her out of their house.

She took Garrett from the bed and gently placed him in the crib. She decided to let him sleep in his shorts and T-shirt and just took off his little shoes and socks.

With him settled for the night, she changed from her slacks and blouse into her nightgown. Breaking a man's heart was exhausting business, she thought as she turned out the light and then crawled into bed. Especially when that man was nice and respectful and should have been a good match for her.

But it was just what Grant had said. Emotions like

love or desire couldn't be forced. They were either there or they weren't, and she knew that no amount of dating Grant would have made those kinds of feelings magically appear.

She fell asleep with thoughts of Grant in her head and awakened the next morning after erotic dreams of Nick. She rolled out of bed at dawn and went right into the shower, hoping to scrub the fevered heat of her dreams, of him, from her skin.

For all she knew, Nick had some honey down in Texas whom he'd spent the past two years with, a woman who might eventually wind up here in Grady Gulch. Not that Courtney cared if Nick had been with a thousand women in the past two years.

The way he'd left town, the way he'd left her had forever scarred her heart and soul. There was no room for forgiveness.

It was almost ten when she had Garrett dressed and ready to head to the park to meet Nick for his hour of playtime with his son. She wore the black T-shirt with the yellow words Cowboy Café across the front and a pair of jeans that was considered her uniform.

As she stepped out of her motel room door, she nearly tripped over a rather large box that sat just outside the door. "What the heck," she muttered. She carried Garrett back into the room and pulled the box inside.

It was a plain, brown packing box, but it had Garrett's name printed in black marker on the top. She opened the box and stared in surprise at the toys inside. They were all new, expensive and age appropriate. She searched the box to find a card or a note that might tell her who had left them for her son but found nothing.

She had a feeling she knew who they had come from. Grant. Was this some sort of last-ditch effort to get her to change her mind about breaking up with him? Was this a reminder of what Garrett could have, what she could have, if Grant remained in their lives?

If Grant's intention was to drive her back into his arms, it wouldn't work. Garrett was happy with the cheap, plastic toys that she could afford to buy him, and she wasn't about to be seduced with material things back into the arms of a man whom she knew in her heart could never make her happy.

"Bye-bye," Garrett said as he clung to her leg.

"I know, just a minute," she replied as she dug her cell phone out of her purse. She quickly punched in Grant's cell phone number. He would probably be in his office at the bank at this time of the morning.

He answered on the second ring. "Courtney!" His voice held a ray of hope.

"Hi, Grant. I just wanted to thank you for the box of toys, but you know given the circumstances between us that I can't accept them from you."

There was a long silence that created a faint anxiety in the pit of her stomach. "Courtney, I don't have any idea what you're talking about. What toys?"

"You didn't leave a box of toys for Garrett in front of my motel room door?"

"It wasn't me. Maybe you have a secret admirer, or maybe it was Nick." His voice was cool, whispering of the fact that he was hurt and still more than a little angry with her.

"Then I'm sorry I bothered you." She clicked off with Grant, the feeling of uneasiness rising just a bit. She stared at the box of toys.

"Bye-bye," Garrett said in obvious impatience.

"Just one more minute," Courtney said as she called Nick. She couldn't let it go. She had to know this minute who had given the toys to Garrett. Although Nick was a logical choice, this ninja night drop just didn't feel like his style.

He answered on the first ring. "Where are you?" he asked. "I'm waiting at the park."

"I know, I'm sorry. We're on our way now. I just need to know one thing. Did you leave a box of toys for Garrett outside the motel room sometime last night or this morning?"

"No, why? Does Garrett need toys?"

"Never mind, I'll talk to you when I see you in about ten minutes." She hung up the phone, and the anxiety in the pit of her stomach exploded.

She didn't like it. She didn't like it at all. It felt wrong. Garrett would not play with those toys until she found out who had given them to him and why.

As she loaded Garrett into his car seat in the back of her car, she found herself looking around the parking lot, feeling the same kind of prickly sensation that had chased her out of the park the day before, the same sense of panic the night she'd awakened and seen the shadow move outside her window.

Grant had mentioned the possibility of a secret admirer. The very thought churned her stomach. Had Candy thought she had a secret admirer before she wound up dead in the cottage behind the café? What about Shirley? Had she received a gift of some sort from a secret admirer who had then crawled in through her bedroom window and killed her?

Stop it, she commanded herself. Stop thinking crazy. There was absolutely no way to tie an unexpected box of toys with two murdered women. There was no way that the crazy feeling of being watched in the park the other day had anything to do with anything. There was absolutely no reason for her to feel threatened in any way.

And yet she did.

Chapter 7

Nick had awakened on the wrong side of the bed, having dealt with a very drunk Adam for half the night. It had taken him hours to finally get his brother in bed, and now Courtney was late.

He leaned against the side of his pickup, his hat pulled low on his forehead against the morning sun and his foot tapping impatiently as he checked his watch for the third time in the past five minutes.

It was already after ten and she'd only given him an hour with Garrett to begin with. He drew in a breath and released the edge of irritation that had been with him when he'd rolled out of bed. He'd deal with Adam later, for now he just wanted to spend quality time with his son.

What was up with the crazy phone call he'd just received from Courtney about toys for Garrett? If Garrett needed toys then Nick would be glad to get him some. If Garrett needed anything, Nick was all-in for being the provider.

The Bensons had never really had to worry about finances. Their parents had stockpiled money that Sam had invested well after their deaths. Between the crops and the livestock, the ranch was in the black each year.

Not that it mattered, but two years of work and no play in Texas had also provided a fairly healthy bank account for Nick. He knew things had to have been financially tough on Courtney, but now he was here to help share that load.

He stood up straighter as her car pulled into the parking lot. "About time," he said as he approached the car. She pulled Garrett from his car seat, but instead of greeting the tall man who was his father, Garrett made a beeline for the sandbox, his diapered butt beneath the jean shorts waddling back and forth with each step.

"Guess I know where I stand on his list of priorities," Nick said with a touch of humor as Courtney pulled the diaper and tote bag out of the backseat.

"Definitely sandbox, Mom and Sophie at this point. But, given time maybe you'll move into third position," Courtney replied.

As she started after her son, Nick followed her, trying not to notice how her tight jeans cupped the shape of her butt, how her rich, dark hair swung freely on the top of her shoulders with each step she took.

He knew her hair would smell of vanilla. Jasmine and vanilla were the scents he would always identify with her, and they would always stir a heat of desire in the center of his belly.

He hurried to catch up with Garrett, passing Courtney just behind him. He couldn't think about her. This was all about a father's right, about visitation with the son he needed to know, who needed to know him.

"Hey, buddy," Nick said to Garrett, who looked up and gave him a happy grin.

"Toys," Garrett said and pointed to the sandbox.

"That's right. We're going to play with toys in the sandbox," Nick agreed. "And speaking of toys." He waited for Courtney to catch up with them. "What was the phone call about?"

Her green eyes darkened. "When I got ready to walk out the door a little while ago, there was a box with Garrett's name written on it. Inside were several brand-new, expensive toys. There was no note to indicate who had left them."

"Probably Hubert," Nick said, trying to ignore the surprising jab of jealousy that shot through him.

"No, it wasn't Grant. I called him and asked and he said he didn't leave anything. And there's really no reason for him to do something like that, because I broke things off with him last night."

Nick looked at her sharply. "Why? I thought he was probably the man of your dreams, the well-off, respectable guy who could help you heal things over with your parents."

"Nothing is going to heal things over with my parents," she said with a fervency that surprised him. "I don't want to heal things with my parents, and my breaking up with Grant had nothing to do with that. And it certainly had nothing to do with you."

They'd reached the sandbox and Garrett stopped at the edge and looked at Courtney expectantly as he obviously needed help stepping over the lip of the sandy play area.

"Here you go, son," Nick said and gently lifted the

boy and placed him in the sandbox. Garrett smiled in delight and tried to grab Nick's hat.

"Whoa." Nick dodged the attempt. "Hat," he said. "This is my hat, but I don't think I want it filled with sand."

"Hat." Garrett parroted. "Toys."

Courtney placed the sand toys into the box and then took a seat at the nearby picnic table while Nick lowered himself to the side of the sandbox and grabbed one of the shovels to start filling a pail.

Garrett grinned up at him and began to help by using another shovel. For a few minutes the two worked together, and when the pail was full, Nick emptied it and they began the game again.

It was surreal, playing in the sand with his son, a little human being he hadn't known existed a day before. He marveled at the shape of Garrett's meaty hands as he filled his bucket, the bright intelligence that sparked in his eyes, and he embraced the laughter that escaped each time Nick emptied the bucket.

"So, why did you break up with Grant?" he finally asked.

"Because I knew that he was looking for more than I could give him. Because I realized it wasn't fair to lead him on when I didn't have any real romantic feelings toward him. And just so you know, I'll repeat it again—it absolutely had nothing to do with you."

"Didn't think it did." Nick should have been ashamed by the sense of satisfaction that swept through him at her words. He knew it was wrong to not want her for himself, but also hate the idea of her being with anyone else.

As Garrett began to cover one of his chubby bare legs with sand, Nick started to cover his other one.

Garrett started giggling, and the sound was infectious. Soon Courtney and Nick were laughing as well, and it felt good.

There had been nothing but tension between them since the moment he'd come back into town, and this moment of shared joy with their son filled his heart with a warmth he hadn't felt since the death of his sister.

It didn't last long, but as he and Courtney shared a last smile over Garrett's head, for the first time since returning to Grady Gulch Nick felt as if he was where he belonged.

For just a brief, shining moment, he wanted to go back in time, back before Cherry had died, before he'd left Grady Gulch, back to the time when Courtney had been his.

He wanted to go back to those moments in the old Yates barn when he and Courtney had spun fantasies of love forever and building a family and supporting one another through good times and bad.

For just a brief moment he wanted it back, he wanted her back, and his need for her filled him up so much that he couldn't think of anything to say when the laughter finally ended.

He spent the next thirty minutes focused on Garrett, playing in the sand, showing him how to fill the back of the plastic pickup truck with the white grains and then pretend to drive it around the sandbox. Garrett mimicked his actions, grinning at Nick with young pride.

"You like working at the café?" he finally asked to break the silence that had grown between them.

"Actually I do enjoy it," she replied. "Oh, I don't like the time I have to spend away from Garrett, but I like the people I work with and I absolutely adore Mary."

He gave her a quick smile. "Everyone adores Mary.

She's one of the best things that ever happened to Grady Gulch."

"She's certainly been good to me. I showed up in the café with a suitcase and a sob story, and she helped me instantly."

He didn't want to think about that time in her life, that time when she'd had to have felt so alone.

"Now that I'm here I can make things easier for you," Nick said. "Maybe you could cut down on some of your hours at the café."

She shook her head. "I take care of myself. I don't want you or any man taking care of me." She raised her chin a notch. "I spent too many years letting my parents take care of me, and in my experience help always comes with strings attached. I'm doing fine, Nick. Garrett and I are doing just fine."

He looked at her somberly, still fighting the crazy feelings that he knew he shouldn't be feeling. "But you know that you can come to me for anything you need, anything Garrett might need. I intend to start paying child support immediately. You just tell me what you want, and I'll pay each month until we work out the custody agreement."

Her eyes once again darkened, as if she didn't even want to think about a custody agreement. "Maybe a hundred dollars a month? It would help with the diapers."

"We'll make it three hundred a month. I'm sure he's outgrowing his clothes with each minute that passes, and if he's like his dad and his uncles, he probably has a healthy appetite. I'll have a check ready for you tomorrow."

He thought she was going to protest, but at that moment Garrett poured a bucket of sand over Nick's head.

Garrett's laughter rode the air as Nick jumped up and pulled his hat off. "Hat," Garrett said proudly.

Nick couldn't help but see the smile that threatened at the corners of Courtney's lush lips. He wanted to capture just one corner with his own mouth, feel that smile expand against his own.

"Courtney," a voice called from the distance.

Both Nick and Courtney looked in the distance, where Abigail Swisher and her best friend Susan May-field headed toward them. Susan's four-year-old daughter, Ella, ran ahead of them, obviously focused on the sandbox.

Courtney got up from the table and Nick brushed the sand from his hair and shoulders as the two women approached. "Nice to see you both," Susan said.

"Garrett! What a big boy you're getting to be," Abigail exclaimed, her smile warm as she gazed at him. "And such a handsome young man."

"Thanks, and he is growing like a weed," Courtney agreed. "And now it's time to get the big boy out of the sandbox so I can get to work."

"I'll get him," Nick offered. "I already feel like I've been in a sandstorm." He leaned forward and picked Garrett up in his arms.

He noticed Abigail staring with an unsettling intensity first at him and then at Garrett. He had a feeling by the end of the day there wouldn't be anyone in town who didn't know he was Garrett's biological father.

Goodbyes were said, and together he and Courtney fell into step walking toward their vehicles. "I think the cat is out of the bag," he said.

"What do you mean?"

"Abigail was giving me and Garrett the eye. By the

time you get to the café, everyone in town will probably know I'm Garrett's daddy."

She shrugged her slender shoulders, and he couldn't help but see the weight of her breasts shift with the movement. "At this point it doesn't really matter. Sooner or later everyone was going to know anyway."

"Does it bother you?" A tightness filled his chest.

"That you're his father?"

"No, that everyone will know that we were seeing each other two years ago."

They had reached her car. She held out her arms to take Garrett from him. "Kind of water under the bridge now, don't you think?"

He watched as she carefully buckled Garrett into his car seat. As she straightened he realized he was standing too close to her. He could smell her intoxicating perfume, see the bright gold speckles in the depths of her green eyes, and again his desire to pull her into his arms, to kiss her lips hit him full force.

For an achingly long moment they remained frozen in place. He was vaguely aware of the heat emanating from her body, a heat he had wrapped himself in for seven wonderful months, a heat he wanted to pull against him this very minute.

She broke the mood, stepping sideways toward the driver door. "I've got to get going. Same time, same place tomorrow?" she asked.

He nodded and moved back so she could get into her car. As he watched her pull away, he told himself he was a fool. To want her. To try to recapture what he'd believed they'd once had.

Two years ago he hadn't been enough for her, and nothing had changed to make him more acceptable since then. He was still just a cowboy rancher, only now he had a brother in jail, another brother who was a borderline alcoholic and a ranch that needed more than a little bit of TLC.

Funny, he knew she was bitter toward him for leaving without a backward glance, but despite his desire for her he realized he had more than a little bit of bitterness still gnawing inside him.

He still believed that eventually she'd date and marry a fine, successful and respectable man like Grant Hubert, a man who would be everything her parents had wanted for her. Eventually she'd be welcomed back into the fold of her mother and father, and that would only make things more difficult for him.

He got into his pickup and headed back in the direction of the ranch, a foul mood taking hold of him as he realized there was a part of him that was angry. He was mad that Courtney's love for him in those seven months they had shared had never been real or strong enough for her to step out of the shadows beside him.

And even knowing that, what really irritated him was that he wanted what he could never have, the woman he'd thought had existed in the straw-scented stable of the old Yates barn, a woman who had only ever existed in his imagination.

Rusty was having a temper tantrum. The cook at the café rarely showed any emotion, but when he got angry it was a sight to see. He banged pans, cussed like a sailor and threatened anyone who dared enter the kitchen for any reason.

Courtney had no idea what had set him off this time, but she stood next to Mary at the counter, waiting until the storm passed. "I don't know why you let him get away with this," Courtney said softly to Mary.

Thankfully the lunch rush had ended before Rusty had blown up.

Mary smiled. "I put up with him because he doesn't do this often, he's a great cook and hard worker. Plus today is the ten-year anniversary of the day he lost his wife and his son in a house fire."

Courtney gasped in shock. "Oh, my God, I didn't know."

Mary nodded. "He doesn't talk about it much. Apparently faulty wiring started a fire in the kitchen while his wife and little boy slept upstairs. Rusty was working nights at a diner and wasn't home when the incident happened. By the time he got there the house was engulfed. It took half a dozen firemen to keep him from trying to enter the inferno to save his wife and little boy."

A dark symphony of emotion rose up inside Courtney as she thought about the kind of loss Rusty had suffered in his life. "How old was his son?" she asked.

"Just about Garrett's age," Mary replied.

"I can't imagine that, losing a loved one, losing a child like that," Courtney said.

"Sometimes Rusty just needs to bang pots and pans and curse to vent a little of the sadness inside him. But he doesn't want anyone feeling sorry for him. It's a tragic part of his life he doesn't even like to talk about."

Within a few minutes silence once again reigned in the kitchen, indicating that the storm had passed, at least inside the café. Outside, the gray clouds had delivered a light rain off and on since Courtney had gotten up that morning.

For the past week she and Nick had met in the park for his visits with Garrett, but this morning they'd met in her motel room because of the weather.

The park visits had been fun, and she'd been reminded of the carefree side of Nick. He'd wrestled with Garrett in the grass, pushed him on one of the baby swings and talked to him as if he was a grown-up.

Despite her tumultuous feelings about Nick even being in Garrett's life, she couldn't help the way her heart warmed when she saw him with Garrett. He would be a terrific father if he'd just stick around.

She'd forgotten about Nick's innate gentleness. She knew his strength, both physical and mental. She'd seen him angry and knew he never backed down from a fight he considered right. Still, she'd definitely forgotten how his eyes could soften with love, how his touch could be as tender as butterfly wings, and as she saw him that way with Garrett it set up a deep yearning inside her.

She felt as if there had been no softness, no gentleness or true laughter in her life for the past two years. The last twenty-four months of her life had been all about survival, something her parents hadn't taught her. She'd taught herself all she'd needed to know except how to spend time with Nick and Garrett in a motel room.

This morning the visit was uncomfortable. The setting had been far too intimate, the space too small, and she'd been too aware of Nick not just as Garrett's father, but as a sexy man she'd once made love with.

She'd watched his arm muscles bulge as he lifted Garrett and remembered how those arms had felt around her. As he'd played patty-cake with Garrett, she'd remembered how Nick's hands had felt sliding down her naked body, touching her with a fire that had made her gasp in delight. Definitely she preferred the outdoors for his parental visits.

Today she'd actually let him take Garrett to Sophie's.

It had been a leap of faith for her, to allow anyone to take her son anywhere without her. She felt a little guilty for calling to check in with Sophie, who had assured her that Garrett had arrived safe and sound.

It was just before the dinner rush began that Lizzy Wiles came in and took a seat at a table in Courtney's section. "Can you take a short break?" she asked when Courtney stepped up to take her friend's order.

Courtney looked around. "Sure, I can sit for a minute or two. What can I get you?"

"Just a tall glass of iced tea and a gossip check-in."

As Courtney went to get Lizzy's iced tea, she knew that she wanted to know what was going on with Nick. Lizzy and Courtney had become good friends immediately after Candy Bailey's murder. Lizzy had been the only one in town who had known that Nick was Garrett's father.

"So, tell all," Lizzy said as Courtney delivered her glass of iced tea and then slid into the chair opposite her. "He's back, he knows about Garrett and I've heard through the grapevine that the three of you have been seen together at the park every day."

"True, true and true," Courtney replied.

Lizzy took a sip of her tea, a dainty frown pulling together in the center of her forehead. "You know you have to tell me more than that," she exclaimed.

"He wants joint custody."

Lizzy's whiskey-colored eyes widened. "Did you expect that?"

"Not in a million years." Courtney leaned back in her chair. "He's really good with Garrett, Lizzy, but it's only been a little over a week."

"Has he told you why he left town?"

Courtney shook her head. "And I haven't asked him.

It doesn't matter. The only thing that matters is the two of us working out the situation with Garrett."

"I also heard you broke things off with Grant. I imagine a lot of people in town will find it odd that you broke up with Grady Gulch's most eligible bachelor a day or two after Nick showed up back in town."

Courtney sighed. "I know, but I realized that even though Grant is a nice man, he was never going to make my heart beat faster, he was never going to make me long for him to kiss me, to hold me. We had no sexual energy between us, and that's important, isn't it?"

Lizzy gave her a wry grin. "You're asking me? A woman who gave up all her plans for her future alone because a sad and lonely cowboy looked at me and made my knees weak, made me want to haul him into bed as quickly as possible? That sexual energy is part of love, and as far as I'm concerned, without it all you really have is a great friendship."

"And that's exactly what I felt like I had with Grant, a friendship that was never going to really blossom into anything else."

"What about Nick? How does he make you feel after all this time?"

Courtney felt the heat that rushed into her cheeks. "It doesn't matter what he makes me feel. I still don't trust him to stick around for the long haul, and I can't forgive him for leaving me before."

"Too bad. You don't get those kind of overwhelming feelings of need too often. I had them with Daniel the moment I laid eyes on him. Somewhere deep in my heart I needed him, even though I did my best to fight against it. Living in Grady Gulch wasn't in my plans, but all it took was one kiss from Daniel to change my life."

Lizzy had been on a trek around the country after her mother's death when she'd landed in Grady Gulch. Her plan had been to spend a couple of weeks working as a waitress in the Cowboy Café and then move on. But, Daniel Jefferson had changed her plans, and now the two were talking wedding.

"I don't need Grant or Nick in my life," Courtney said. "I was doing fine before either of them came along, and I'll be fine without them. Still, I have to admit seeing Nick with Garrett makes my heart melt a little."

Lizzy nodded. "Little boys need fathers. Nick tried to apologize to me for his brother's attack."

Courtney was vaguely surprised. "He did?" The Nick she had known in the past didn't particularly like confrontation, and she suddenly realized how hard it must have been for him to return to his hometown with everything that had happened, with everything that was happening in his family.

"Of course I told him an apology was unnecessary. It's so much healthier to look forward instead of back. Looking back only mires you in places and events you can't change."

Courtney nodded. "I'm taking all of this one day at a time, with no expectations."

"While you're doing that, you should probably work on the anger and bitterness that's been inside you since Nick left."

Lizzy gave Courtney one of her bright smiles. "But, you know me, I don't believe in hanging on to negativity. It eats you from the inside out."

"Point taken," Courtney replied.

"You are being careful, aren't you?"

Courtney frowned. "Don't worry, I'm not having sex with Nick."

Lizzy laughed but sobered quickly. "I wasn't talking about safe sex. I was talking about your personal safety. These murders have me spooked for you and everyone who's working here."

"I'm spooked too, but yes, I'm being careful." She didn't mention the creepy-crawly feelings she'd had in the middle of the night or at the park. Thankfully, nothing had happened in the past week to make her anxious or experience that strange panicked feeling. She'd written off those moments as part of her anxiety about Nick.

Lizzy checked her watch. "And now I'd better let you get back to work. I promised Daniel I'd only be in here a few minutes. He's waiting out in the car. He knew I just wanted some girl talk."

"The iced tea is on me," Courtney said as they both got up from the table. They gave each other a quick hug, and then Lizzy disappeared out the door and Courtney got back to work.

The evening rush lasted longer than usual, making it impossible for her to think of anything except getting orders and seeing to the needs of her customers.

Right before her shift ended, a group of teenagers came in, filling several tables.

Mary had just let Lynette go home, and so Courtney agreed to stay later than usual to take care of the exuberant teens. She made a quick call to Sophie to let her know that she'd be a little late to pick up Garrett, and then she got back to work serving the teens, who were a fun and raucous bunch.

By the time they finally left, Courtney was exhausted. She grabbed the glass of iced tea she'd fixed herself before the dinner rush began and took a couple of quick sips. The ice had melted long ago and the tea was room temperature, but at least it was wet.

She carried her glass and joined Mary behind the counter and gave her boss a tired smile. "That was a fun group, but I can't say much about their tips."

Mary laughed. "Unfortunately the youth of this town doesn't understand the twenty percent rule for good service."

Courtney smiled wryly. "I would have been happy with ten percent and fewer gum wrappers."

"Thanks for staying so late."

"Not a problem," Courtney replied. "Any news from Cameron on the murders?"

"No, and it's eating that poor man alive. You are being careful about locking up when you're at the motel?"

"Definitely," Courtney assured her. "And there are people constantly coming and going there. But, a strange thing happened the other morning. A box of new toys was left in front of my door with Garrett's name written on it."

"Grant or Nick?" Mary asked.

"Both of them said they didn't leave the toys."

"Rumor has it that Grant isn't happy about the breakup, that he's angry with you and hurt."

Courtney's heart gave a twinge of sadness. "I'm sorry about that. The last thing I wanted to do was hurt him, but I knew in my heart he wasn't the man for me. He was here during the dinner rush, but didn't sit in my section and didn't even make eye contact with me."

"Ouch." Mary winced, then continued, "Maybe the toys came from some well-meaning person who knows how much you struggle to make ends meet as a single parent. You know what they say, don't look a gift horse in the mouth."

"Actually, I dropped the box off at the Methodist

church. I figured there might be somebody who needs them more than Garrett. It just felt too weird to have toys for him that I didn't know where they came from."

Mary nodded. "I'm sure somebody will find them useful. And now, speaking of Garrett, get out of here and go pick up your son. Give him a hug for me, and I'll see you tomorrow at noon."

"Okay, have a good rest of the night, and tell Cameron I said hello." Courtney knew the lawman always ended his night here at closing time. She also knew that something simmered just beneath the surface between Cameron and Mary, but as far as she knew their relationship hadn't crossed the boundary of friendship.

She downed the last of the tea and then carried her glass into the kitchen and loaded it into the industrial-size dishwasher. As she headed toward the door back into the dining area, a wave of dizziness momentarily stopped her in her path. She steadied herself and drew a deep breath. Apparently she was more tired than she'd thought.

With a final good-night to Mary, she stepped outside into the dark, wet night and thought of Mary and Cameron. They would make a perfect couple. She frowned. What did she know about perfect couples? She didn't want to think about anyone else's relationship. She was having enough problems sorting out her relationship with Nick.

During the past week, as she watched him play with Garrett, there had been moments when she couldn't reach for her anger where he was concerned, where the bitterness had been buried by shared laughter.

She loved watching Nick play with his son, but she didn't want to love him again. She had told Lizzy the truth. She didn't trust that he was in for the long haul, and she refused to put her heart on the line for him again.

As she walked across the lot toward her car, another wave of dizziness caused her to stumble and she banged into the driver's side door of her car.

"Wow," she muttered to herself. She shook her head in an effort to clear a faint fog that had set in. She got into her car and locked the doors, a weary sigh blowing from her lips. She just wanted to pick up her son and not think about Nick or anything else until the next morning.

The rain that had bothered the area for most of the day was present again, peppering down on her windshield enough that she had to turn on her wipers.

Tonight she wished Sophie lived closer, in town rather than down a dark country road. Although Sophie's house was only a fifteen-minute drive from the café, tonight she knew it would take a little longer.

Tired. A nearly overwhelming drowsiness claimed her as the rain came down in earnest and the narrow, dark road appeared to undulate before her.

The swish of the windshield wipers across the window was hypnotic along with the road that appeared to shift and sway before her eyes.

A seductive darkness edged in around the perimeters of her consciousness. She shook her head in an attempt to dislodge the darkness. But it refused to go away.

Her eyes drifted closed, but she quickly snapped them open. She was vaguely aware that there was a sharp curve coming up. She had to get somewhere... Where? Where was she going? She couldn't remember.

The darkness that had flirted at the edges of her consciousness swooped in, and she knew no more.

Chapter 8

Nick leaned back in the leather recliner chair in the spotlessly clean living room and breathed a sigh of tired relief. Adam had left that morning to spend a couple of days with a friend in Wichita and check out some horses he was considering purchasing.

He'd had to use some heavy persuasion to get Adam to leave, but Nick thought the trip would be good for him. Adam needed some time away with friends, a place where he could forget about Sam for a little while. Hopefully he would return with glimmers of the old Adam present.

The minute Adam had left, Nick had dived into a cleaning frenzy the likes of which the old house hadn't seen in months. He'd started in the kitchen and worked his way through the entire lower level of the house.

Nick frowned as he thought of his eldest brother. He'd talked to Sam today, who had called from the

Oklahoma City jail, where he was being held until his trial. It had been a painful and awkward conversation.

The trial was still months away, but Sam showed no signs of regret or remorse for what he had tried to do to Lizzy Wiles. The man Nick had spoken to hadn't even sounded like the Sam he knew. There had been such hatred, such rage in his voice, and Nick had been left with the certainty that unless something changed between now and the trial, Sam would be spending a long time in prison.

Nick picked up the remote and punched on the television to fill the silence of the big house. The silence felt sad. It whispered of a family torn apart by tragedy and loss, by anger and madness. Where there had once been six, two parents and four children, there were now only two.

Funny, in the two years he'd spent in Texas he'd been basically alone, but he'd never been lonely. It was only in this house, where the sound of his sister's laughter lingered in the very walls, where the shadow of Sam sat in the study, that loneliness was found.

As the ten o'clock news came on, he thought about Courtney. She was probably snuggled down in bed now with Garrett asleep in his crib. The time he'd spent with Courtney and Garrett over the past week had been both an intense pleasure and filled with a longing he didn't want to address.

Garrett had already crawled deep into his heart with his goofy grins and easygoing nature. He was quick to throw his arms around Nick's neck now, but Nick wasn't sure if the attraction was Nick himself or his black cowboy hat.

Courtney was a different matter. Nick didn't want her in his heart again. It didn't matter that circumstances had changed, that she no longer had to worry about her parents' approval of whom she dated. The sting of the past remained with him, coupled with a sharp desire to pull her into his arms and kiss her until her lips were red and swollen.

There was no question that he was conflicted about her, and he knew the best thing to do about it was maintain some emotional distance from her.

As the news ended, he switched to a sitcom in an effort to shove thoughts of Courtney out of his head. When the sitcom was over he remained in his chair, trying to decide if he wanted to go on to bed or stay up for a little while longer.

He jumped as the house phone rang. He was so accustomed to using his cell phone, he'd nearly forgotten they had a landline. Wondering who would be calling at this time of the night, he got up from his chair and went to the sofa, near where the phone sat on the end table.

"Hello?" he answered.

"Nick, this is Sophie."

Instantly Nick's stomach churned as he thought of Garrett in trouble. "Sophie, what's up?"

"I'm not sure what to do. Courtney called earlier and told me she'd be a little late to pick up Garrett, but she still isn't here. I called the café and Mary told me she left well over an hour ago."

The churn of his stomach exploded into full-blown anxiety. "Is Garrett okay?"

"He's sleeping now, but I'm worried about Courtney," Sophie said. "She's never done anything like this before. She always comes here to get Garrett directly after work."

"I'll check things out and call you right back," he said, fighting against a panic that pressed tight against his chest. He hung up and immediately punched in Courtney's cell phone number. It rang four times and then went to voice mail.

Where would she be at this time of night where she couldn't or wouldn't answer her telephone? What would keep her from picking up Garrett as she usually did immediately after work?

Nick hung up the phone and grabbed his car keys from the kitchen table. He hesitated at the front door as he watched the rain come down. Where could she be? Ducking his head, he raced from his front door to his truck, deciding that the best place to start looking for her was the café.

It took two tries to get his keys in to start the ignition to the engine. His hands shook and his thoughts scattered in a million different directions.

All kinds of scenarios flew through his head. Two women working as waitresses had been murdered. Maybe her car had skidded off the road. Why didn't she answer her phone? Maybe she and Grant had met up somewhere for a reconciliation.

He told himself he didn't care if that was the case, that all he really cared about was that she was okay. When he reached the café through the sheet of rain that fell, he didn't see her car in the parking lot.

He braked and tried her phone again, and once again it rang and then went to voice mail. "Courtney, where are you? Sophie called me and is worried about you. Call me when you get this message."

There was only one road that would lead her toward Sophie's ranch house and he exited the café parking lot to head in that direction.

He drove slowly, the rain a definite impediment to visibility. The road was dark and rain-slicked, and he tried not to think about the night that his sister, Cherry, had taken off, driving too fast for the weather conditions, driving to her death with her best friend in the car.

This night has nothing to do with that night, he told himself. That night it had been an early sleet mixed with snow that had slickened the road, not a hot July rain. Cherry was known for driving far too fast, and Courtney was a cautious woman who shared little in common with his wild, reckless sister.

He drove slowly, searching the sides of the roads, wishing his cell phone would ring and she'd tell him that bucket of junk she drove had broken down and she was at Buck's Auto or she'd gotten a wild hair and was at The Corral having a couple of drinks with some of the other waitresses.

Even as he thought of these things, he dismissed them. If she'd had car trouble she would have called Sophie, and Courtney definitely wasn't the kind of woman to put having drinks with friends over her son.

She was in trouble. He felt it in his heart. He felt it in his very soul, and he needed to find her as quickly as possible.

As he approached the curve ahead, he twisted his head from side to side, checking the road for her car. He stomped on the brakes and squealed to a stop. Through the curtain of rain down the dark embankment on his left, he thought he saw a faint light glowing.

There were no houses there, no reason for a light of any kind to be shining unless it was a taillight of a car. Thankfully the rain had ebbed somewhat as he got out of the vehicle and focused his gaze on the light, trying to discern exactly what it was in the darkness of the night.

He reached back into his pickup and grabbed the flashlight he kept in the glove box and then, with his heart pounding like the hooves of a running stallion, he slid down the slick embankment toward the small glow.

It was a car.

It was her car.

As he drew closer he saw both back lights, one of them half-hidden by a thick bush.

"Courtney!" he cried as he slipped down the wet grass toward the driver's door. He wrenched it open and gasped as he saw her as still as death, slumped over the steering wheel.

With a cold, trembling hand, he gently touched the side of her neck, praying for a pulse at the same time he fumbled with his other hand to get his cell phone out of his pocket.

He gasped in relief as he felt the faint beat of her pulse against his fingers, then punched in 9-1-1. It took him only a minute to call for an ambulance and the sheriff and give his approximate location.

As he waited he leaned into the car, afraid to touch Courtney, afraid to try to move her but needing her to wake up, to tell him she was okay.

"Courtney, everything is going to be all right. I've got help coming. Hang on." He had no idea if someplace in her mind she could hear him or not.

Damn. Her car was so old there were no air bags, nothing but a worn seat belt that had obviously not worked well enough to keep her from banging her head.

"Courtney, can you hear me?" How long had she been out here unconscious? Fear slithered through him as he thought about what little he knew about head injuries.

All he really knew was that he wanted her to wake up right now and talk to him, let him know that she'd bumped her head but she was going to be just fine.

He breathed a sigh of relief as he heard sirens coming closer with each jagged breath he took. He nearly collapsed in the grass as the ambulance arrived, followed by Sheriff Evans's patrol car.

"Down here!" he yelled as the paramedics jumped out of the ambulance and Cameron approached Nick, his hand holding a big-beamed flashlight. "She's unconscious," Nick said to the sheriff. "She must have hit her head, and I can't get her to wake up."

Cameron grabbed Nick by the arm and moved him back from the car so the paramedics could get close enough to attend to her. "She must have slid off the road in the rain," Nick babbled. "Sophie called me to tell me Courtney hadn't picked up Garrett and she was worried about her. I came looking and happened to see her taillight shining down here in the dark."

Cameron nodded. "Maybe she hydroplaned and lost control going around the curve."

Nick glanced over to where the paramedics were loading Courtney onto a stretcher to carry her up the embankment and to the awaiting ambulance. "God, Cameron. She's got to be all right."

"Go on," Cameron said and pointed to where they were loading Courtney into the ambulance. "You go with her and I'll take care of things here."

Nick didn't need to be told twice. He raced up the embankment and back to his truck and within minutes was following the emergency vehicle carrying Courtney to the hospital.

"She has to be okay," he said aloud to himself as he gripped the steering wheel tightly. She'd looked so still. What if she'd hit her head too hard? What if she never woke up?

Don't jump to conclusions, he told himself as he

parked in the hospital parking lot and raced for the emergency door. Right now the most important thing was Courtney getting the medical help she needed.

As he waited in the lobby for word on her condition, he called Sophie to update her on the situation. "As soon as I find out how she's doing, I'll call and come and get Garrett," he said.

It was nearly an hour later that Dr. Andrew Spiro entered the lobby. Nick jumped up out of his chair to greet the doctor. "She's still unconscious. She's definitely suffering a concussion, among other bumps and bruises. We've x-rayed her head, and I see nothing to indicate that she's in any real danger. I'm keeping her overnight for observation."

"Can I see her?" Nick asked.

Dr. Spiro nodded. "She's in room 110. Please limit your visit to a couple of minutes."

Nick was already halfway down the hallway before the doctor had finished his last sentence. The room was in semidarkness and Courtney was a tiny, fragile figure amid the large hospital bed with the pristine white sheets.

He sank into the chair close to the bed, his heart thudding wildly as he gazed at her. "Courtney, I just want you to know that you don't have to worry about Garrett. I'll take good care of him until you're better. I've already arranged with Sophie to pick him up, and I'll take him home with me tonight. I can keep him as long as necessary. You just need to wake up and let me see those beautiful eyes of yours." She didn't move and he had no idea if his words had penetrated through or not.

A nurse arrived at that moment to take Courtney's

vitals, followed by Dr. Spiro, who shooed him out of the room with the comforting words that she would be fine.

By the time Nick arrived back at the scene of the accident on his way to Sophie's, Courtney's car was being pulled from the embankment by one of Buck's tow trucks. Thankfully the rain had stopped, and Nick got out of his truck and approached where Cameron and Deputy Ben Temple stood watching the action.

"Can I get the baby seat out of the car when it's on firm ground?" Nick asked, thinking that he needed to buy one so he wouldn't have to depend on transferring Courtney's back and forth.

Cameron nodded. "Should be just a minute or two now. How's she doing?"

"Still unconscious. Dr. Spiro told me she has a concussion but they took some X-rays and he's assured me she's going to be all right. I just wish she would have regained consciousness while I'd been there."

"She must have hit her head pretty hard. That seat belt didn't do anything to halt her forward progress when she slammed into that tree." Cameron frowned. "Old clunkers like these without air bags should be banned from the streets." He drew a deep sigh. "I'll probably write this one up as a weather-related incident unless something comes up to warrant a full investigation."

"As if you don't have enough on your plate already," Nick said drily.

"My murder investigations are getting colder by the day." Disgust laced Cameron's voice.

Minutes later as Nick left the scene with Garrett's car seat in the back of the king cab of his pickup, his thoughts returned to Courtney. Hopefully by now she was awake. She was going to feel like hell for the next couple of days, but at least she'd been lucky. This kind of head-on crash could have killed her. His stomach clenched tight at this thought.

Sophie met him at the door with the sleeping Garrett in her arms. "Courtney will be okay?" she asked worriedly.

"Dr. Spiro assured me she's going to be just fine, but I'm sure she won't be at work for the next couple of days. I'll keep in touch with you and let you know how things are going."

As she transferred the sleeping child to Nick's arms, his heart filled with love as Garrett snuggled against him as if he knew he was where he belonged.

Sophie also handed him a large diaper bag that she said should see him through the night as far as diapers and necessities were concerned.

Nick gently carried his son to the truck and buckled him into the car seat, grateful that he had supplies that would at least get them through the night. He had no crib, so Garrett would sleep with Nick in his bed. Nick would probably not get a wink of sleep for fear the little boy would wake up and wander around.

A million thoughts whirled around in his head as he arrived at the ranch and carried Garrett and the diaper bag into his bedroom. He tenderly placed Garrett into the center of the king-size bed and then closed his bedroom door so that at least if he woke up at some point and Nick was asleep, Garrett couldn't escape the bedroom.

He moved the chair in the corner of the room so its back was against the far side of the bed, hoping it would provide an adequate barrier so Garrett wouldn't roll over in his sleep and fall out of the bed.

Nick shucked his clothes at the side of the bed and

laid his hat on the nightstand. Clad in his boxers, he got into the bed next to the sleeping child.

For several long moments he kept the bedside lamp on and just looked at Garrett, taking in the puckered little lips, the long, dark lashes that dusted his chubby cheeks, the cleft in his chin that marked him forever as Nick's.

He drew in a deep breath, smelling the scent of his son, a powdered-little-boy scent that halfway stole his breath away.

Love welled up inside Nick, a kind of love he'd never felt before. He would fight to the death for this child. He would work his fingers to the bone, do whatever it took to keep his son happy and healthy.

He would be the father to Garrett that his own hadn't been to him. He'd demonstrate his love to Garrett by touch, by kiss, by word and by deed. Garrett would never doubt how deeply he was loved by his daddy.

He rolled over on his back and stared up at the ceiling, thinking of the accident and Courtney.

His emotions toward her were so ambivalent. He'd always care about her as the mother of his child, but despite his desire to the contrary, his feelings for her went deeper than that.

When he thought of the past, a seed of bitterness still lingered deep inside him, but when he thought of the past week they had spent together, that seed could find no sustenance, no way to flourish.

The idea that she was hurt ached inside him. She'd looked so small, so still, when he'd seen her in the hospital. A fierce protectiveness had surged up inside him. He never wanted to see her hurt like that again.

A deep exhaustion swept over him, not only the mental exhaustion of the worry and fear he'd suffered earlier, but the tiredness of a full day of cleaning inside the house.

At least Courtney was okay, although by tomorrow she'd probably have aches in places she didn't know she possessed. It was the last thing he thought before sleep claimed him.

He awoke suddenly, blinking at the light that he'd forgotten to turn off before he'd fallen asleep. He turned his head to see Garrett, sitting up and grinning at him, Nick's hat hanging crookedly on his head.

"Hat!" Garrett said proudly.

Nick frowned, wondering how the kid had gotten the hat from the nightstand without falling either over Nick or on his own head.

Garrett tumbled forward and grabbed Nick by the nose. "Nose," he announced.

Nick grinned. "Yes, that's my nose and my hat." He sat up and pulled Garrett's fingers away from his nose and his hat off the boy's head. He glanced at the clock. Just a little after three. "And now it's time to sleep," Nick said.

Garrett closed his eyes, a delighted smile on his rosebud lips. "Sleep," he said dutifully. His eyes flicked back open. "Wake!"

There wasn't a trace of sleepiness in Garrett's bright blue eyes. Rather, there was the mischievous glint of a child ready to play.

Nick fought against a tired yawn as he realized it was going to be daddy trial by fire. And the first challenge was what to do with a fully awake little boy in the middle of the night.

Chapter 9

Courtney hissed inwardly as she awoke to the morning sun shining through the nearby window. Disoriented and confused, she looked around the room. It was obvious she was in a hospital, but how did she get here? Why was she here?

She raised a hand to her pounding head, and her arms ached as if she'd fought a hundred rounds in the ring with a professional boxer. Her chest hurt, too, and she felt as if her brain had been wrapped in cotton.

Garrett! If she was here, then where was her son? She fought against a sense of wild panic as rational thought slowly made its way through her foggy head.

If she was in the hospital, then that meant people knew she'd been hurt. Nick and Sophie would both know, and one of them would make sure that Garrett was taken care of.

Nick had probably taken him home. Would he know

how to feed him? Would he be able to handle the little guy for an entire night?

Would he get a clean diaper on right? What would he do if Garrett cried? A glance at the clock on the wall let her know it was just past six. Too early to call Nick, because if Garrett was sleeping she didn't want to wake him.

"Ah, it's good to see you're awake," Dr. Spiro said as he entered the room. "You've had us all a bit worried because you were unconscious for so long. How are you feeling?"

"A bit groggy. I have a headache. I feel like I've been run over by a truck. Other than that I'm okay. What happened to me?"

"You don't remember?"

"I have no idea."

Dr. Spiro wrapped a blood pressure cuff around her arm. "Sometimes that happens with a head injury. You were in a car accident and you were brought in last night." He pumped the cuff. "You suffered a concussion, among other things. You have a bruised chest, and your knees were banged up. Overall, you're going to feel like heck for the next couple of days." He released the pressure on the cuff and watched the dial.

"Good," he said as he unwrapped the cuff. "Blood pressure is normal. Can you tell me your name, the date and who the president is?"

She rattled off the information and Dr. Spiro grunted in satisfaction. "What you need most now is rest. Your body has been through a trauma. I'll leave you alone now and you relax. Somebody will be in within an hour or so with some breakfast." With these words he left her room.

So, what had happened to her? She frowned, ignoring the pain that sliced through her skull as she tried to remember the events of the night before. Why couldn't she remember the accident?

She had no answers and she must have fallen back asleep, for when she opened her eyes again Dr. Spiro was at her side, asking her if she felt up to talking to Cameron.

It was just after eight, and even though she wanted to call Nick and check on Garrett, she had to trust that her son was safe in his father's care. Cameron was here to talk to her now, and there was no question that she wanted some answers from him.

"I'll bet you're feeling pretty rough this morning," Cameron said as he came into her room, a sympathetic expression on his face.

"And that would be an understatement," she replied and tried to force a smile, but the simple gesture shot pain through her aching head.

"You want to tell me what happened last night?" Cameron said as he sat in the chair next to her bed.

"I was hoping you could tell me," she said drily.

He frowned. "You don't remember the car accident?"

"Not at all," she replied. "Dr. Spiro said that with a concussion sometimes there's also a bit of temporary amnesia about the event."

"So, what do you remember about last night?" Cameron asked.

Courtney searched inside for anything she could remember that had happened the night before. "I remember working at the café. A bunch of teenagers came in at the last minute, and so I stayed later than usual to help Mary. One of the boys tipped me in gum wrappers."

Cameron smiled, but the smile lasted only a moment. "And after that?"

She thought back, desperately trying to retrieve any memory that she might possess. A frantic kind of panic threatened to crawl up the back of her throat as she stared at Cameron. "And after that, nothing. Dr. Spiro told me I went off the road and wrecked."

"Head first into that big old tree at the base of the embankment just off the curve," Cameron explained. "You were lucky you weren't killed instantly."

Courtney fought off a shiver of what might have been. She might have never seen Garrett again, she might have never had the opportunity to see him grow, to watch him become a man.

"You don't remember getting into your car?"

"No, I don't," she replied.

"Had you had anything to drink?"

"Cameron, you know me better than that," she exclaimed. "Number one, Mary doesn't serve alcohol. And number two, I would never drink and drive."

Cameron held up his hand. "I know, but I had to ask."

"So, what happens now?" she asked. "Are you going to write me a ticket or something?"

"For what? For speeding? If you were, I wasn't there to see it. I'm writing it up as a weather-related accident and that will be the end of it. Your car has been towed to Buck's, and I have to tell you the damage is pretty extensive."

She nodded, ignoring the banging in her head. "I'm sorry I can't help you more. I just don't remember anything," she said, and then her heart lifted in joy as Nick appeared in the doorway with Garrett in his arms.

"Mama!" Garrett exclaimed with a happy grin.

Cameron nodded to Nick and then looked back at Courtney. "I've got what I need, but if you think of anything else give me a call. And now you just need to get better."

As Cameron went out the door, Nick came in. A quick once-over of her son let her know he looked as happy and healthy as he had the last time she'd seen him. The only thing she noticed was that his little white T-shirt was on inside out.

Nick, on the other hand, looked as if he'd had a rough night. His eyes were bleary with lack of sleep, his hat looked as if it had been mauled by a rabid dog, and dark whiskers covered his lower cheeks and chin.

"Good morning," she said. "Rough night?"

"Probably no rougher than yours." He sank into the chair Cameron had vacated as Garrett reached up and pulled his hat from his head.

"Hat," Garrett exclaimed as he put it on his own head, the brim falling down to his nose. "My hat," he said, his voice muffled. Nick took the hat off Garrett's head and set it on the floor.

"This kid is obsessed," he muttered. "And how are you?" His tired eyes gazed at her with a tenderness that suddenly made Courtney want to cry.

She swallowed against the impulse. "I'm okay. Definitely sore all over, but my head is feeling better and I'm hoping to get out of here by late this afternoon. You look tired."

"I am," he confessed. He pulled a couple of little toy cars from his pocket and gave them to Garrett, who immediately began to use Nick's muscled arms as a highway. "He woke up at three this morning and decided it was time to play. I tried to get him to go back to sleep, but he was having nothing to do with it until about five this morning. Then he slept until seven, and here we are."

"Has he had any breakfast?" Courtney asked worriedly.

"Two eggs scrambled, a half a piece of toast, a little sausage and a sippy cup of milk," Nick replied. "Did you think I was going to starve him to death?"

"Of course not," she replied, realizing that she'd underestimated Nick's abilities where Garrett was concerned.

"I even managed to diaper the right end several times," Nick added with a small smile.

Once again Courtney felt the press of tears at her eyes. She didn't know if her raging emotions were because of the physical trauma she'd suffered or the fact that she knew without a doubt Nick would make a terrific father.

But for how long? She somehow felt as if they were in a honeymoon period, but sooner or later the honeymoon would end and real life would intrude.

It was obvious Garrett was already attached to Nick, but he was still young enough that if Nick walked away tomorrow there would be no scars. But, what about two months from now? Six months from now?

She couldn't worry about that at the moment. In truth, she had no control over Nick's future plans, good or bad, for Garrett. "If you give Sophie a call I'm sure she'd be able to watch him for the rest of the day. That way you could go home and get some rest until I get out of here and can take back mommy duty."

"We'll be fine." Nick grinned at Garrett. "I figured we'd go to the park and play for a little while and then maybe have lunch at the Cowboy Café."

Courtney looked at him in horror. "I've got to call Mary. She'll be expecting me at noon today."

"I already took care of it. I told her you'd be off today

and then after the weekend we'll see how you feel about going back to work on Monday."

She tried to work up some anger that he had gotten into her business, but she couldn't. She was just grateful that it had been taken care of. At least it was Friday and she would be losing only today's work. Surely by Monday she'd feel fine.

"Then after lunch we'll come back here and check in with Doc Spiro to see if he's going to release you today," Nick continued.

"Oh, he's going to release me today," she said firmly. "I'm not spending another night here."

Nick grinned teasingly. "And you're the boss, right?"

"That's right," she replied lightly. "And don't you forget it."

Nick stood and leaned over her with Garrett in his arms. "Kiss Mommy," he said.

As Garrett laid his lips against Courtney's forehead and smacked, she fought the impulse to pull the little boy into her arms. But her chest was so sore and her head still ached, and she knew a wiggling little boy would only make her feel worse.

"We're off to the park," Nick said as he straightened.

"Toys?" Garrett asked.

Nick nodded. "Toys, and you rest," he said to Courtney. For just a brief moment his eyes darkened as he held her gaze. "You scared the hell out of me, Courtney. When I found you in that car unconscious...I've never been so terrified. For a minute I thought we'd lost you."

She saw the depth of emotion that shone from his eyes, and it pulled forth the crazy longing she fought against each time they were together. "I'm here now, I'm fine, and by the time you have lunch and get back here, I'll be more than ready to go home."

With a quick flurry of goodbyes, they were gone and Courtney remained staring at the doorway, wishing she was going with them to the park. But, to be honest, all she wanted to do was stay in bed and rest her wickedly aching body.

It was odd, that she had been so afraid of Nick finding out about Garrett's existence and it had taken only a little over a week for her to feel completely confident with Garrett in his care.

She hadn't expected Nick's love for Garrett. She hadn't expected it to be such a visceral thing in him, but that's what she saw whenever he looked at Garrett.

Was it enough to keep him in Grady Gulch? Was Garrett enough for Nick to change his ways and become the man she'd once believed him to be? That remained to be seen.

She thought again of the night before and tried to tamp down the lingering fear that had set up residency inside her. The lack of any memories at all of the night scared her.

What if it hadn't been some sort of temporary amnesia from the accident? What if she'd blacked out for some other reason? What had happened to her that would steal all her memories of a significant period of time?

The rest of the morning and the early afternoon passed quickly. Several visitors stopped in to see her. Lizzy and Daniel arrived with a bouquet of summer flowers, Abigail Swisher brought a plate of homemade chocolate chip cookies on a red paper plate with a pink doily, and even Junior Lempke's mother, Lila, arrived with a handmade card that Junior had made for her.

Courtney managed to visit and let everyone know

that she was fine, but the worry about the missing memories simmered deep inside her.

It was after two when Nick and Garrett returned, and as Garrett played with a new toy that Nick had bought for him, Nick and Courtney made small talk while they waited for Dr. Spiro to write up her dismissal papers.

"I'm finding it hard to wrap my head around the fact that I can't remember anything from last night," she said.

"You took a pretty hard knock to the head," Nick replied.

"I know, but if it was just a concussion, why was I unconscious all night long? Something feels off. Something feels wrong about the whole thing."

Nick studied her intently. "What do you mean? What do you think happened?"

Just that quickly Courtney's head began to bang again. She raised a trembling hand to her forehead as she tried to make sense of it all. "I don't know. I'm sure Dr. Spiro is right and it's just a result of the accident."

"If Spiro is letting you go today, then you're coming home with me," Nick said with a firm voice that defied her to argue with him. "You're obviously still in pain and you need somebody not only to take care of Garrett but to take care of you."

She felt too sick both physically and mentally to protest. Besides, she wasn't at all sure she wanted to be alone right now. Even if the doctor was right about the temporary amnesia thing, that didn't take away the pain in her head, the ache in her arms and her overall feeling of being beaten half to death.

"Can we go by the motel and get some of my things?" she asked.

Nick nodded and she saw the vague surprise in his

eyes. Under any other circumstance she would never agree to go with Nick to his ranch for any length of time, but at the moment she recognized she was too beat up to properly care for Garrett, and she felt too vulnerable to want to be alone.

It was almost six o'clock by the time Courtney was released from the hospital. They made the trip to the motel to pack up a suitcase for her and Garrett, and Nick loaded Garrett's crib and high chair into the back of the pickup.

"It's crazy to be bringing all of this for a night," Courtney said as they headed toward the Benson ranch house.

"It will just make things easier on all of us if Garrett has his own bed and high chair, even if it is for just one night," Nick replied.

"It *is* just for one night," she replied.

He shot her a quick grin. "Because you're the boss, right? Yeah, boss, well we're going to play this one by ear. Even though you're putting on a good show, I can tell that you're hurting. A couple of days of TLC will be good for you."

"We'll see," she said, refusing to commit to more than a single night.

"You've been busy," she said as they reached the ranch and she saw the neatly cut lawn and trimmed shrubs.

"Yeah, it was in pretty bad shape. Slowly but surely I'm making some headway on cleaning things up." He parked the truck and opened the driver's door.

"Tell you what, why don't I go inside and draw you a hot bath and while you soak, Garrett and I will unload things and start on some dinner," he said as he pulled Garrett out of his car seat.

She was shocked by his kind offer. Who was this man who stood before her, her son in one arm and a gentle caring in his blue eyes?

The man she'd fallen in love with two years ago had displayed a touch of youthful arrogance, a cockiness she'd found both thrilling and sexy. But, this man who stood before her was even sexier as he talked of baths and babies and making dinner.

"A hot bath sounds lovely, but I'll help you carry things inside before I'll think about a bath."

It didn't take them long to get Garrett's crib set up in a guest room, which had a full bed covered in a buttercup-yellow spread. Nick started running the water in the tub in the bathroom across the hall while Courtney unpacked the few things she and Garrett would need for the night.

"Ready for me to add the bubbles?" Nick asked. Garrett toddled at Nick's side, gibbering in the language of presentences that only he understood.

"Bubbles?"

Nick appeared in the bathroom doorway with a bottle of strawberry bubble bath in hand. "This belonged to Cherry. I'm assuming bubble bath doesn't go bad."

"I'd love some bubbles," she replied, touched that he would allow her to use his sister's bubble bath. "Where's Adam?" she asked. She hadn't seen Nick's brother since they'd arrived.

"Adam is out of town for a couple of days. He's visiting some friends and checking out a few horses we might purchase."

"Oh." When she'd agreed to come here for the night she hadn't thought that it would be just herself, Garrett and Nick in the big house.

"Worried about your reputation?" he asked, and she thought she detected a sharp edge to his words.

"Of course not," she replied. "I was just wondering why I hadn't seen your brother, that's all."

He nodded. "I'll go finish up your bath."

A half an hour later Courtney lay in the scented bubbly water in the bathtub and finally felt her sore muscles begin to relax.

She leaned her head back against the cool porcelain and closed her eyes, trying to keep her mind as empty as possible. But, no matter how hard she tried, she just couldn't think of nothing.

It wasn't thoughts of the accident that scurried through her head; she had no memories of getting into her car, of driving on the rain-slicked streets and flying off the road and into the tree.

Why? Why couldn't she remember leaving the café? She could understand losing the memories of the initial impact and being unconscious, but she didn't remember even telling Mary goodbye the night before when she'd left the café.

And if that wasn't enough for her to think about, thoughts of the man in the kitchen with her son filled her brain.

What had he been doing for the past two years of his life? She knew he'd been working on a ranch, but what had he done besides that? He seemed to have arrived back in her life with no baggage from that time.

She'd certainly had baggage. She'd had Grant. She frowned as she thought of the man she'd broken up with only a week earlier. He'd come into the café during the dinner rush the night before although he hadn't sat in her section, indicating he was still angry with her for breaking up with him.

Why could she remember him coming in to eat and the teenagers leaving her a paltry tip, yet she couldn't remember walking out of the door to get into her car?

It was this troubling thought that finally pulled her out of the tub. She dried off with a large fluffy towel that Nick had provided and then looked at her reflection in the mirror.

There was some slight bruising at her hairline on her forehead, but thankfully it wasn't creeping downward. Her sternum had a faint discoloration from contact with the steering wheel. All in all everyone was right—she'd been tremendously lucky to walk away from the accident.

She pulled on a pair of pink shorts and an oversized navy T-shirt, deciding that her bra would be too uncomfortable, then went in search of Nick and Garrett.

She found them in the large country kitchen. Garrett, seated in his high chair munching on a cracker, greeted her with a wide smile.

Nick stood at the stove, stirring something in a large pot. He turned and gestured her to the table with a smile. "Something smells good," she said as she sat at the large oak table.

"Ground beef, jarred sauce and spaghetti noodles that are slightly overcooked," he replied.

"Sounds yummy. Can I do anything to help?"

"Nope, just sit there and look pretty and I'll do the rest." He left the pot on the stove and reached into a cabinet for two plates and a plastic bowl. He set the plates on the table and handed Garrett the bowl. The boy promptly put it on his head.

Courtney took the bowl from his dark curls and placed it on his high chair tray. "It's not a hat," she said and touched his little nose.

"Hat," he said and pointed to Nick.

Nick added silverware to the table and smiled. "He definitely has a hat fetish."

Courtney smiled. "If you think his hat fetish is funny, wait until you watch him eat spaghetti. You might want to break out the hazmat suits."

"How much mess could one little boy make with a bowl of spaghetti?" Nick asked.

A half an hour later as he wiped sauce off the floor and then a nearby cabinet, he shook his head ruefully. "Who would have thought," he said more to himself than to Courtney, who was clearing the dishes from the table. "I've never seen spaghetti fly before."

She laughed. It had been nearly impossible to carry on any kind of conversation through the meal as Garrett had been a pip, finding the game of throwing pasta as entertaining as eating it.

He now sat in the high chair, face cleaned and properly contrite after being fussed at by Courtney for his bad manners. "How about I make some coffee and we all go into the living room?" Nick suggested once the kitchen was clean.

"That sounds nice." As Courtney attempted to lift Garrett from the high chair, her bruised and sore muscles protested.

"Here, let me do that," Nick exclaimed. "How about you make the coffee and I'll take Mr. Garrett in and dress him in his pajamas."

Once again Courtney was shocked by what a natural Nick was at parenting. As she made a short pot of coffee, she thought about Nick the daddy.

She hadn't expected him to be so demonstrative with the child. He kissed Garrett often, ran a hand lovingly through his curls. The light of love in his eyes when he gazed at the boy was obvious and seemed to grow brighter each time father and son were together.

He'd once seduced her as the taboo bad boy, but if she wasn't careful she'd find herself equally seduced by the father in him.

By the time she carried two cups of coffee into the living room, Nick had a pajama-clad Garrett on his lap on the sofa. "I think somebody has had a long day," Nick said.

"Are you talking about yourself or Garrett?" she asked teasingly.

"He didn't have much of a nap today and he almost fell asleep while I was changing him."

"Maybe we should just go ahead and put him down for the night," she said, although she wasn't so sure she liked the idea of being totally alone with Nick without the buffer of Garrett between them. Then she was irritated with herself for even thinking she needed a buffer between herself and Nick.

Fifteen minutes later Garrett was asleep and Nick and Courtney were back in the living room seated on the sofa with their coffee.

"Tell me about Texas," she said. "You pretty well know what I've been doing for the past two years, but what did you do down there?"

He leaned back against the sofa, looking sexy and relaxed. "I've got a friend down there named Charlie Hanes. He hired me on at his ranch, and that's what I did for the past two years. I worked, I slept and I ate, and I like to think that during that time I did a little growing up."

He took a sip of his coffee and then continued. "I'd never really been alone before. There was always a sibling to pick up the slack if I got too lazy, somebody to tell me what to do, to party with or to just talk to if I felt like it. I'd never had to depend just on myself. I'd never really taken the time to look inside and find out what was there."

"And what was there?" she asked with curiosity.

He shot her a lazy grin. "I'm still a work in progress."

And she liked the way he had progressed. There were still flashes of the boy he had been when he'd left Grady Gulch, but there was more substance, more solidness to him now.

"In lots of ways I think I've grown up, too," she replied. "For the first time in my life I suddenly not only had to depend on myself, but also had to think about how I was going to take care of a baby. And I'm proud of how I've managed to do both without anyone's help."

"You've done a great job," he replied, and his eyes held a soft light that felt seductive.

She suddenly felt the need to distance herself from him. He seemed like an illusionist to her, playing havoc on her senses, on her very sensibilities with his magic. She took a big drink of her coffee and then stood.

"I think it's been a long day for me, too. I'm exhausted and I need to call it a night."

He got up as well and set his cup on the coffee table next to hers. "Courtney, before you go…" He stepped close…closer still to her, and her heart began to beat a rapid rhythm.

He stopped when he stood so close to her that she could feel his body heat and was engulfed by the heady scent of him. "Yes?" she asked, her mouth dry.

"I've been wanting to do this the minute I yanked open the car door and saw you slumped over the steering wheel." He wrapped his arms around her and gently pulled her toward him.

She stood stiffly in his embrace for just a brief moment and then yielded to the warmth and familiarity of him, gave in to her need to have strong male arms around her. Melting against him, she released a tremulous sigh.

He felt just as she remembered, big and safe and warm, and she was in no hurry to leave his arms. She nestled her head into the crook of his neck and was reminded of how well their bodies had always fit together. His heart beat against her own, a steady, strong rhythm that further relaxed her.

It had been a long time since she'd felt the comfort of anyone's arms around her, and she hadn't realized until this moment how hungry she'd been for this kind of physical contact.

It felt right to be in his arms and she would have stayed there forever, but he took his finger and raised her chin so she was looking up at him. His blue eyes were dark with unabashed desire, and she knew he wanted to kiss her.

And even though she knew a kiss from Nick was wrong on all kinds of levels, she wanted it. She wanted him. She opened her lips slightly, as if to invite him to take what he wanted from her.

He lowered his head and claimed her mouth with his. Initially his kiss was feather-soft against her lips, heating her from her head to her toes. He deepened the kiss, touching first her lower lip with his tongue, and then delving inside her mouth with desire and determined intent.

She raised her arms to his shoulders and pressed more tightly against him as their tongues swirled in heated battle. She'd forgotten his kiss.

She'd forgotten how when he kissed her she felt as

if he touched her all over, as if kissing was the most important thing in the entire world. Nick's kisses had always been infused with not just desire, but also with caring, making her feel like the most important woman on the face of the earth.

"You know I want you," he said as he finally broke the kiss. His voice was deep with need.

Would it be so terrible? To make love with him just one last time? It wouldn't mean anything, because she refused to allow her heart to be involved with him ever again.

Just one more time to hold in her heart for when he eventually got tired of playing daddy, when he ran from his family responsibilities not just to Garrett, but to the ranch and Adam, as well.

Fool, a little voice whispered in her head at the same time she placed a hand on the side of his cheek. "I want you, too."

She didn't want to dwell on their past, and she didn't want to contemplate the future. She just wanted to be in this moment with him, feeling safe, feeling desirable and fooling herself into believing that she was loved.

Chapter 10

Nick wasn't sure exactly what he expected from Courtney, but it wasn't the shine of desire in the depths of her eyes, it wasn't the words he'd most wanted to hear.

He took her hand and led her down the hallway toward his bedroom, afraid with each step that somehow the mood would shatter, that she'd change her mind.

The last time he'd been with her he'd been consumed with grief and despair. This time he wanted to make love to her with joy and the fullness and wonder of life between them.

When they reached his room, she paused in the doorway and dropped his hand and for a moment he was certain she'd changed her mind. And if she had he was okay with that, although his need for her burned bright and hot through him.

"You know this won't change anything between us," she said, her voice a hoarse whisper. "We're Garrett's parents, but this won't make you be anything more in my life."

"All I'm asking for is this night," he replied. Could she hear his heart? Pounding with such an intensity that it seemed to fill the entire room? Could she feel his need, so intense it left him almost breathless?

His answer seemed to satisfy her, for she took several steps toward him and once again buried herself in his arms as their lips met in a fiery kiss.

As their kiss lingered he gently caressed her slender back as her full breasts pressed evocatively against his chest. The scent of her stirred him on every level, evoking old memories of making love with her and heightening his anticipation to repeat the intimate act.

When his hands reached the bottom of her T-shirt, he slid them beneath and caressed upward against the warm bare flesh of her back. "Take it off," she whispered as she stepped mere inches away from him.

She didn't have to ask him twice. He grabbed the bottom of the T-shirt and pulled it over her head. He tossed it to the nearby chair and then gazed at her beauty. Her breasts were definitely fuller than he remembered, a residual effect of her pregnancy.

"Now take yours off," she said.

He smiled at her. "Yes, boss." He pulled his own T-shirt off and they came together, bare skin against bare skin.

"You've always felt so right in my arms," he whispered as he moved his lips down the slender column of her neck.

Her only answer was to drop her head back to allow him full access to her throat. He loved the way she tasted, but it wasn't long before he wanted more…more.

He stepped away from her and tugged her toward the

bed, mindful that he needed to be gentle with her because of the physical trauma she'd suffered two nights before.

She stopped by the edge of the bed and stepped out of her shorts, leaving her clad only in a wispy pair of white panties. Nick nearly came undone. Never had he seen her so sexy, and he hurriedly shucked his jeans, tore off his socks and yanked down the navy bedspread to expose the white sheets beneath.

It all felt like a dream to Nick as he slid under the sheets next to her. This was a dream he'd entertained since the moment he'd first met her. To have her, to hold her, not in the confines of a stable in the old Yates barn, but rather in his own bed in his own house.

She moved back into his arms, the only barrier between them her little panties and his boxers. Their bare legs entwined as their lips met once again.

Her skin was soft and silky, just as he remembered, and he wanted to touch her everywhere. He felt the need to hurry, as if at any moment the dream would shatter and she'd jump up and run out of his room.

Forcing himself to take his time, he broke the kiss and instead moved his lips once again down her throat, across her collarbones and to the erect tip of one of her breasts. As he teased and flicked, she tangled her hands in his hair, as if in an attempt to pull him closer… closer still.

There was no talk. The room filled with the sound of sweet sighs of delight, deep moans of desire, and that was all the communication necessary.

His hands remembered where she loved to be stroked, his mouth knew where she was most sensitive, and by touching, by kissing there he would elicit an intense response from her.

He not only loved making love with her, but making love *to* her. His desire was to give her the most pleasure, to give her moments she would never forget, to somehow mark her as his own for the rest of their lives.

Still, she was certainly not a passive participant. She took off her panties and then yanked his boxers off him. Nick was on fire and ready to possess her, but he had no intention of doing so until she had enjoyed a climax.

He slid his hand down her stomach, below her hip bones and to the place where he knew his touch could bring her the most pleasure. She sucked in a deep breath as he placed his fingers intimately against her.

Every muscle in her body stiffened as he increased his movements against her, and her back began to arch, letting him know the waves of pleasure sweeping through her were about to peak.

She began to shudder, a low deep moan escaping her lips as her climax claimed her. It was only when the last of her shudders had left her that he moved on top of her.

He was as hard as a rock; ready to take her hard and fast, but he also didn't want this all to end so quickly. He slid into her and hissed a sigh of pleasure as he felt her completely surround him.

He felt as if he was home, and he closed his eyes to fight for control. It was at that moment he realized he'd never stopped loving Courtney.

She'd been in his heart, in his soul since the moment he'd let her go and left Grady Gulch. Even though he'd tried to move on, she was still as firmly implanted in his heart as she had been the day he'd left.

Moving against him, she arched her hips to meet him thrust for thrust. He kept his rhythm slow, wanting to stay inside her forever, but as she gripped his buttocks with her hands and urged him to go faster, his control snapped.

Together they moved in a frenzy until she cried out with another orgasm that sparked his own. Moments later they lay gasping to catch their breaths.

"Some things just get better with age," he finally said as he stroked a strand of her dark hair.

There had been a time when he'd believed he knew what she was feeling, what she was thinking, but as he gazed down into her green eyes, he realized he had no idea what was going through her mind.

"I'm on birth control pills," she said, making him realize that he hadn't even considered any kind of protection. "And I haven't been with anyone since the last time we were together."

"I haven't been with anyone since then, either," he confessed. She looked at him dubiously. "It's true, Courtney, and to be perfectly honest, I wouldn't have minded another slipup between us if the result was another boy like Garrett or a little girl like you."

Again he found it impossible to read her. She didn't reply but slid away from him and off the bed. She grabbed her panties from the floor and then disappeared into the adjoining bathroom.

Nick stared up at the darkened ceiling, the only illumination in the room spilling in from the hall light. Without her presence next to him his thoughts went to dark places.

Despite the fact that he wanted her physically, that he was still as in love with her as he had been two years ago, he couldn't forget that she was now back in his life for two reasons: Garrett and the fact that she no longer had a relationship with her parents.

Neither life-altering event had been of her own

choosing. If Garrett hadn't been born, she probably wouldn't be here with him now. She wouldn't be seen with him on a date or at her work. As much as she'd once professed to love him, she'd never chosen him over the approval of her parents.

And on the day he'd needed her most, as his precious sister had been buried, she hadn't been standing by his side. Rather, she'd been at a tea party her mother had given for her little-town society friends.

He shook his head, as if mentally dislodging the bitterness of the past. His body was still warm from hers, and her sweet scent lingered on his skin. He didn't want to think about anything but what they'd just shared.

He turned his head as she came out of the bathroom, a dark wraith in white panties. "Are you okay?" he asked, wondering if maybe he'd hurt her during their lovemaking or something he said had upset her.

"I'm fine. Just tired."

"Want to hang around and cuddle for a little while? As I recall, you were always a great cuddler." He was hoping to pull a smile to her face, and to put some distance between himself and his momentary negative thoughts about the past.

They were here now, and that was all that mattered. They had a son who would keep them bound together in one form or another for eighteen years and beyond.

"I think I'll just head on into my own room with Garrett," she said, disappointing him. He watched her walk to the bedroom doorway, and then she turned and faced him once again. "This changes nothing, Nick. You're my son's father, but I can't allow you to be anything more than that to me."

She didn't wait for his response, but instead turned and disappeared down the hallway. Nick stared after her and wondered why he had even entertained the idea that there could be more between them.

He'd never really been what she wanted, what she needed, and her words were just a reminder of that. Besides, why would he want a woman who had kept him a secret for seven long months, who had refused to take him out of the shadows and into the sunlight?

He knew he wasn't the same man he'd been when he'd left Grady Gulch. During his two years away from home he'd matured, he'd figured out what was important in life and what wasn't.

Unfortunately, he couldn't be sure Courtney had changed at all. Maybe she was still her parents' daughter after all, looking for a man who had the kind of respectability within the community that Nick would never manage to achieve as a simple rancher.

Nick had never been a fool for anyone or anything, and he'd be a damned fool to want anything from her except the coparenting arrangements they eventually made.

Still, despite the fact that she had given no indication that they would ever have a real future together, despite the past that occasionally rose up to burn in his gut, he wanted her. Not just for a night, but for a lifetime, and he supposed that made him all kinds of a fool.

She knew it was a mistake. Being here in his home had been mistake enough, but falling into his arms, into his bed, had been the worst thing she could do.

She got into the bed in the room where Garrett slept peacefully in his crib and stared up at the ceiling. It had been just like she remembered with Nick—exciting and wonderful…sheer magic.

It had been as if each and every piece of their bodies had remembered one another. Everything had been so natural, had felt so right, and she'd wanted to spend the entire night in his arms and awaken still in his bed in the morning.

She'd wanted that so badly it had frightened her. She didn't want to love Nick. She didn't want to depend on Nick. But it would take her a very long time to forget the magic of being in his arms, of feeling his body move intimately against her own.

Even now she could smell the scent of him lingering on her skin, and she wanted nothing more than to get out of her bed and join him in his, to be held by him the rest of the night.

In the time he'd been back in town, he'd definitely surprised her in the way he'd stepped up for her and Garrett. There was a new maturity about him that was as appealing as his easygoing charm.

It would be so easy to fall in love with him again if she allowed herself. But she'd sworn she would never be vulnerable to anyone again, especially a man like Nick.

It had been easy to date Grant, because on some level she'd recognized he'd never own her heart. She hadn't been vulnerable to him and so had felt safe.

Nick made her feel physically protected and mentally threatened, and she knew when morning came she had to leave here. She didn't trust him, but, even more, she didn't trust herself not to repeat the past.

She awoke with the slant of the sun letting her know it was late…later than she'd ever slept since Garrett had been born. The crib was empty, and she knew Nick must have crept into the room to get Garrett before she awakened.

She took advantage of knowing Garrett was taken care of and lingered in bed, her thoughts in turmoil. Bits and pieces of troubling moments whirled through her head... The day in the park when she'd felt as if somebody was watching her and the box of toys that had appeared out of nowhere. And she still couldn't shake the feeling that her missing memories were the result of more than just the car accident.

Had she suffered some sort of blackout, some brain disturbance that she knew nothing about? Was she sick in some way? More frightening was the thought that one of the blackouts could happen again, when she was alone with Garrett.

It was after ten when she showered, dressed and headed into the kitchen, where she heard the sound of Garrett's laughter floating out.

She peeked in to find both of them seated on the floor. Nick had a red plastic colander on his head and Garrett wore a plastic tub that had once held something called Baker's Barbecue Beans.

As she watched, they exchanged "hats," and Garrett giggled with delight. Nick caught sight of her and patted the floor next to them. "Look, here comes Mommy." He held out a lightweight green plastic mixing bowl. "And here's Mommy's hat."

Courtney had left the bedroom with every intention of telling Nick she was heading home and packing things up. But, as she looked at her son, whose big blue eyes were filled with mirth, and Nick, whose eyes twinkled with humor, she suddenly wanted to join in their make-believe world.

"Mommy, hat!" Garrett exclaimed and then giggled once again as she plopped down on the floor next to him and placed the mixing bowl on her head.

"Does this strike you as a little bit ridiculous?" she asked Nick.

He shrugged his shoulders and grinned. "I guess in the privacy of my own kitchen it's okay to be a little ridiculous with a fifteen-month-old. Oh, and this is kind of like a game of musical chairs. When he claps his hands and points, we change hats."

As if on cue Garrett clapped. The colander went on Garrett's head, the mixing bowl on Nick's and the bean container to Courtney. Garrett laughed so hard he tipped backward, kicking his feet in the air with amusement.

They played the game for about ten more minutes and then Garrett finally got bored and began to stack the containers. "How about some breakfast?" Nick asked as he got up from the floor and held out a hand to help Courtney up.

"I'm not really that hungry. Actually, there's something I want to talk about," she replied. She moved to the coffeemaker and poured herself a cup, aware that she could be further complicating her life if she told him her fears.

"Okay, but are you sure you don't want some breakfast? I can whip up a couple of eggs for you."

She shook her head and instead took a sip of the coffee. He joined her at the table with his own cup of the fresh brew. He eyed her darkly. "If you want to rehash what happened last night, you already made it pretty clear where things stand between us."

"No, that's not what I want to talk about. I've been racking my brain all morning about this amnesia thing. I told you that I didn't feel like it was necessarily related to the accident. I started wondering if I'd blacked out, if maybe I have a brain tumor or something terrible going on inside me."

Nick looked at her in surprise. "Have you had something like that happen before? Have you blacked out? Missed time?"

"No, nothing like that," she admitted.

"Dr. Spiro told me he'd x-rayed your head. I'm assuming he did a CAT scan or MRI. They would have found a brain tumor or something like that wrong with you."

She nodded. "I agree, and that leaves the last thought that I have about all of it."

"And what's that?" he asked with curiosity.

"I've been thinking about the very last moments before I apparently left the café for the night. I remember serving the teenagers that came in late. I remember them leaving and clearing my section, and then I drank the iced tea that I'd made for myself earlier in the day." She paused and looked at him, wondering if she'd lost her mind.

He raised his cup to his mouth and narrowed his gaze at her. He sipped the coffee and then set the cup back on the table. "So, what exactly are you saying? That somebody put something in your tea?" He looked at her dubiously.

"I know, I must sound crazy." She wrapped her fingers around her cup, wondering if she was just a little bit out of her mind. "I just know that everything was fine before I drank that tea, but afterward, that's when everything went blank."

"But why would somebody do that?"

"I don't know. Maybe somebody thought it would be funny," she replied.

Nick's eyes narrowed dangerously. "Something like that's not funny. I think we should call Cameron and tell him what you think."

She hesitated. "But, I can't know for sure if that's what happened."

"Where was your glass of tea?"

"Where I always keep it, on the little two-top table counter closest to the restrooms."

"So, anyone could have had access to it." He pulled his cell phone from his pocket. "We should at least have Cameron check it out. Did they draw any blood from you that night?"

She checked her arms, since she couldn't remember the hospital visit until she'd awakened the next morning. "No, it doesn't look like it. And the glass I used will have already gone through the dishwasher."

Garrett squealed in delight as his stacked containers fell over. He began the building process all over again as Nick dialed Cameron's phone number.

As she listened to Nick explaining to Cameron why he was calling, she felt a little silly. Was she overreaching? Was the blankness really just a residual effect of the accident, or had somebody spiked her drink with some kind of drug?

"Cameron is going to check into some things," Nick said as he hung up the phone. "He'll get back in touch with you if he has any news."

"Thanks, I don't know if I'm crazy and sending him on a goose chase or not."

"I'd rather err on the side of caution. If you think there's a possibility that you were drugged that night then Cameron needs to know and he needs to find out who is responsible."

She took another sip of coffee and glanced at Garrett, happily playing on the floor. Somebody glancing in the window would see what appeared to be a happy, domestic scene. It stabbed her in her heart and she had the sudden need to escape this place and this man.

She set her cup in the sink and turned back to face him. "I think it's time for me to go home. It's time for me and Garrett to get back to our normal life." Being here with Nick felt almost as dangerous as everything else going on.

Nick looked at her in stunned surprise. "Surely after what you just told me you don't want to go back to the motel today."

"Nobody is going to spike my drink while I'm at home," she replied.

"Stay here and rest. You've got nothing else to do and neither do I. You should use the next couple of days to heal," he protested. "What if somebody did drug you?"

"If they did, then I'm on notice now to be careful and watch who is around me. I feel okay," she replied. She refused to be swayed by his words. She needed to get away from him. Besides, she couldn't stay here forever. She shook her head. "We'll be fine. I want to go home."

"What are you going to do about a vehicle? You don't have any way of getting around."

"I'll rent something for a couple of weeks. I'll be fine," she assured him.

His eyes narrowed slightly. "Is this about what happened between us last night?"

"Yes and no," she admitted. "Nick, I can't play pretend with you. We crossed a boundary last night that we shouldn't have. We need to come to agreeable terms concerning Garrett, but we can't let what happened last night happen again. It's not fair to either one of us."

"But, why can't we?" He raised his voice to be heard above Garrett's banging with a wooden spoon on several pans Nick had put on the floor with the containers earlier. "I don't want you for just one night, Courtney. I want you and Garrett for all my nights and all my days."

The past slammed into Courtney's brain with the force of a hurricane. How many times had she heard him say that same kind of thing in the old barn where they'd spent so much time? How many times had he professed his deep love for her, made her believe they were going to share a future together?

"I can't do it again, Nick." Just saying the words made her heart ache with a sharp pain she hadn't felt since he'd left town two years ago. "I just can't go through the heartbreak of you again."

"I should have called," he said, his voice loud in the sudden silence as Garrett stopped banging on the pans. "I should have called you when I left here." He lowered his voice. "I should have given you an explanation, but I was in such a bad place all I could think about at that time was my own pain and my own needs. I accept that. I accept that I was wrong, but I'm not the same man I was then. I'm not about to run anywhere anymore."

She had waited so long to hear those words from him, had dreamed of him coming back to her...for her. But, the truth of the matter was that he'd returned to Grady Gulch because Sam had been arrested and Adam was in emotional trouble. The truth of the matter was it had been by mere luck alone that they'd reconnected at all. She was confused by him, by her own feelings for him.

"Nick, let's just leave the past to the past. If you don't want to take us back to the motel, then I'll make arrangements for somebody else to come and pick us up."

Although she appreciated the fact that he'd apologized, it didn't take away the small seed of bitterness she'd harbored for the past two years. She'd had twenty-four months to curse his name. It would take longer than a week or two to figure out exactly where he fit in her life…if he truly fit at all. It would take her even longer to believe that he was in this for the long run.

"Fine, I'll take you home if that's what you want." She could tell by his narrowed lips and clipped tone that she'd upset him. But, what she'd told him was the truth. Although she'd always love Nick, sometimes love just wasn't enough.

It took nearly an hour to reload the crib and the high chair and all of the things they'd packed from the motel the day before.

"You want me to take you by Wally's to see about a rental car?" he asked when they were all in his pickup and headed toward the motel.

Wally Simpson had the only car lot in town. He not only sold new and used cars, but on occasion he would rent to somebody when the need arose.

"No, that's okay. I'll call him when Garrett takes his nap this afternoon." She noticed that Nick gripped the steering wheel tightly and that a tension wafted from him that whispered of suppressed anger.

What did he have to be angry about? She was the wounded party in all this. She was the one he'd left behind after promising to love her forever. She was the one who had been left pregnant and alone and had to deal with everything all by herself.

The rest of the ride was accomplished in a tense silence broken only by Garrett's occasional gibberish. When they got to the motel, it took another twenty minutes to get the crib set back up where it had been and the high chair once again in place.

"Thank you, Nick," she said when everything was inside and there was nothing left to do or say.

Garrett was in his high chair, munching on a cracker before she made him lunch, and Nick walked over and kissed him on the forehead. "Bye, son."

"Bye-bye," Garrett replied.

Nick walked toward the door but paused before leaving and turned back to her. "Remember, we don't know if what happened on the highway the other night was an accident or if somebody slipped you a roofie. Please be aware of your surroundings, and don't go anywhere alone." His worry was obvious as he held her gaze intently.

"I'll be careful, Nick. I promise." She couldn't help but be touched by his concern.

He nodded, but it was obvious he had something else on his mind, as he still didn't turn to leave. He leaned against the doorjamb, his hat pulled low. To anyone else he might look at ease, but Courtney felt the tension that rolled off him, saw the way his muscles tightened beneath his black T-shirt.

He tipped his hat back, allowing her to see the simmering blue of his eyes. "Courtney, you weren't the only one who felt left behind in the relationship we had in the past."

She stared at him in stunned surprise. "What are you talking about?"

A muscle began to tick in his jaw as the visible tension rippled through him. "Every time you left that barn, I wasn't sure if you'd ever come back to me. Every time you went back to your privileged life in Evanston with your parents, I wasn't sure that I'd ever see you again."

He drew a deep breath and continued. "You kept me hidden from your friends and family, from everyone in

town for seven long months, like I was a dirty little secret you were too ashamed to admit to. You weren't the
only victim of all this. There were two victims in our
past relationship, Courtney. I was one, too."

He whirled around and before she could respond in
any way he stepped out of the door and closed it behind
him. Courtney stared at the wooden door, shocked by
his words and by the edge of resentment that had laced
those words.

The past and her own anger where he was concerned had been deeply ingrained in her over the past
two years, and now she suddenly felt as if everything
she'd believed to be true was in question.

Somebody may or may not have drugged her iced
tea. Somebody may or may not have been in the woods
in the park stalking her. Her son's father had returned
to claim his rights as a father, and now he'd somehow
managed to make her wonder who had really been at
fault when he'd left her behind and hadn't looked back.

Chapter 11

Courtney awoke after a troubled night of sleep. She'd
tossed and turned most of the night with visions of the
past whirling around in her head. When she'd finally
managed to pull herself out of bed, she felt as if she had
a hangover of unsettled emotions.

After Nick had left the day before she'd contacted
Wally Simpson, who had brought her a rental car.
Thankfully her insurance would also help defray the
cost of the unexpected expense.

She'd also called Mary to let her know she'd be in for
work as usual at noon on Monday. Mary was pleased to
hear she was feeling okay but insisted she give herself
another day before returning to work.

For the rest of the night Courtney had played with
Garrett and done everything in her power not to think
about Nick. She'd gone to bed early but had been
plagued by dreams that had made her feel as if she
hadn't slept at all.

Once she was up and dressed, she spent the morning on mundane tasks, feeding Garrett, cleaning the room and trying desperately not to think about what Nick had said to her the night before.

She wasn't surprised when her phone rang and it was Cameron. "Sheriff," she said in greeting.

"How are you doing, Courtney?"

"Much better today," she replied.

"After speaking with Nick yesterday, I did a little checking this morning. Unfortunately no blood work was done when you were in the hospital, and since something like GHB or Rohypnol is quickly metabolized, no tests would help us now."

"Maybe it was just a stupid idea of mine," she replied, feeling guilty that she was taking his time away from the two unsolved murders he already had on his plate.

"I don't think it's just a stupid idea," Cameron replied. "Mary told me that she watched you head out to your car and you looked like you were drunk, that you stumbled and wove, and she just assumed you were trying to dodge the rain puddles in the parking lot. Now I'm wondering if it was something more than that."

"So, what happens now?"

"What I'd like from you is the name of those teenagers you served right before you left the café. I'd also like the names of anyone you can remember who was in the café for the dinner rush that night. If somebody drugged you and caused your accident, then I want to find who's responsible."

"I appreciate it, Sheriff," she replied. "I know you have enough to deal with right now."

"I don't like somebody murdering people in my

town, and I don't like somebody drugging people in my town," he said forcefully.

"I'm really not sure that's what happened," Courtney replied.

"I still intend to investigate it until we're both satisfied with my findings. You just work on that list and I'll pick it up from you sometime tomorrow. I'll be in touch," he said and then hung up.

Courtney clicked her cell phone closed and thought of the task ahead of her. The café had been busy that night, and it would take some real concentration to make the list Sheriff Evans had requested.

The new possibility that somebody had drugged her definitely made her feel threatened. She didn't believe the teenagers had anything to do with it. None of them had left their booth during their meal or after. They'd eaten and headed straight out the door.

If her drink had been tainted, it had been done sometime during the dinner rush, and the only reason would have been to cause her harm.

Needing somebody to talk to, she finally called Lizzy and the two made a dinner date for that evening at a restaurant in Rockville, the same town Grant had driven them to for the pizza debacle.

Courtney felt a need to escape not just the motel room, but also Grady Gulch for a little while. It was just after six when she loaded Garrett into the rental car and headed toward Rockville. She'd already fed Garrett his dinner because she was meeting Lizzy later than their usual dinnertime.

She figured he'd be asleep in his chair before the meal was over and they headed back home. As she drove out of town she checked her rearview mirror often, aware that the events of the past couple of weeks had definitely created more than a touch of paranoia inside her.

Garrett kept up a steady stream of chatter that kept her entertained and her mind unusually blank as she drove. She didn't want to think, at least not until she could share her thoughts with Lizzy.

It was almost seven by the time she pulled into the parking lot of the Rockville Barbeque. Even with the windows rolled up, she could smell the savory scent of smoky meat and tangy sauce that wafted from the large brick building.

She parked and looked around, seeking Lizzy's car, but she didn't see it anywhere in the lot. "We'll just wait a few minutes for Aunt Lizzy," she said as she leaned over to smile at Garrett in the backseat.

He returned the smile and motherly love swelled up inside her. He'd been an unexpected gift, and she'd never known she was capable of the kind of love she felt for him.

As she turned back around she saw Lizzy's car pulling into the parking lot. "Time to go." As Lizzy pulled into the space next to her car, Courtney got out, grabbed her purse and then opened the back door to get Garrett out of his seat.

"Need help?" Lizzy asked.

"I got it." Courtney pulled Garrett into her arms and then smiled at her friend. "Thanks for meeting me, Lizzy," she said as the two women headed for the restaurant's front door.

"Hey, I always look for an excuse to come here for barbecue, and besides, Daniel had bookkeeping stuff to do tonight, so this worked out perfectly. He gets peace and quiet in the house, and I get burnt ends and baked beans."

Courtney laughed, and within minutes they were seated at a table with Garrett at the end in a high chair. During the meal they talked about the upcoming town festival and Lizzy's wedding preparations. The conversation remained pleasant until they ordered dessert and coffee.

"As much as I've enjoyed having dinner with you, I know you didn't call me to meet with you because you wanted my scintillating conversation. Now, tell me what we're really doing here," Lizzy said.

Courtney frowned. "I just feel like I've been dwelling in my own head for too long and need somebody to talk to about some things."

"That's what friends are for," Lizzy replied as she cut into her gooey piece of chocolate cake. "Now, tell me what's going on."

Courtney picked up her fork and then released a deep sigh. "I'm feeling weird about things."

Lizzy grinned. "And you called me for a reality check?"

Courtney couldn't halt the small smile that crept to her lips. "Crazy, right?" The smile fell away as she stared at her friend.

"What's going on?" Lizzy asked softly.

"It's a bunch of little things that make me feel like maybe I've gone around the bend." She told Lizzy about the day in the park, the strange box of toys for Garrett and then her intuition that she'd been drugged on the night of her accident.

Lizzy listened to everything and then leaned back in her chair. "But what could somebody hope to accomplish by drugging you? I mean, they wouldn't have known for sure when during the night you might have drunk your iced tea."

"True, but I almost always finish up the night drinking the tea. And, maybe it's possible they didn't care when I drank it. Maybe they hoped I'd black out and fall, get hurt or even get arrested for doing drugs." Courtney released a sigh. "Just tell me I'm nuts and I'll try to put this all out of my mind."

Lizzy frowned. "I don't know, Courtney. With the murders of two waitresses from the café still unsolved, I would take all of this pretty seriously. Not to scare you or anything, but what if the killer is toying with you?"

Courtney stared at Lizzy. She hadn't really put it all together in her mind, but hearing it from Lizzy made her realize that very fear had been smoldering someplace deep inside her. Had the killer changed his mode of operation? Had she somehow been targeted as his next victim? The thought was too horrible for her to sustain.

"And then there's Nick," she said in an effort to change one difficult topic to another.

Lizzy nodded, as if unsurprised. "Having him back in town has to have stirred up a lot of old feelings, both good and bad."

"And some new ones, as well," Courtney admitted. She stuck a fork in the cake, but she had no real appetite for the dessert. Her stomach had been upset since the night before.

She sighed and set her fork to the side. "I'm so confused. I've spent the last two years of my life hating him with a passion for leaving me, and then last night he said something that kind of shook me up."

As Courtney told Lizzy about the argument that really hadn't been an argument with Nick the night before, her friend listened patiently without asking questions or making any comments.

"I hadn't thought about how Nick might have felt during the time that we dated," she finally said.

"Why were you secretly seeing him?" Lizzy asked. "I never really understood that. Oh, I get it that you were worried about your parents' reaction to Nick, but he's a good guy and not exactly the devil himself, and you weren't an underage girl."

"True," Courtney admitted. She leaned back against the booth and frowned thoughtfully, remembering that time in her life.

"It all seems so silly now, especially given what's happened between me and my parents since then, but at that time I was so afraid of disappointing them, so afraid of stepping out of the box they'd placed me in, and I knew that Nick was definitely out of that box. I was sheltered and naïve, and even at that age I worried about what my parents might think."

"And what were you afraid might happen if your parents did find out about Nick?" Lizzy asked.

A dry, humorless laugh escaped Courtney's lips. "Exactly what happened when they found out I was pregnant, that they'd stop loving me, that they'd kick me out of their lives." She cut off a piece of her cake and gave it to Garrett.

"Sounds like they were emotionally abusive to you," Lizzy said.

"Of course not," Courtney quickly replied with a sharp gaze at her friend. "They did everything for me. They bought me the best clothing, made sure I had the best parties and ate the best food."

"Those are material things," Lizzy scoffed. "Things that they wanted for themselves. Conditional love, that's what they showed you and as far as I'm concerned that's emotionally abusive. They kicked you out when you needed them most. Can you think of a single thing that Garrett could do that would make you cast him out of your life forever? Anything at all?"

Courtney really thought about it. Certainly there were things Garrett could do that would absolutely break her heart and make her miserable. She thought of Sam, who had tried to kill Lizzy. If Garrett did something so heinous like that, would she throw him out of her life forever?

No, she would want him to face the consequences of his actions, she would want him to get the help or punishment he needed, but she would never stop loving him. If he found himself in trouble, she'd do anything in her power to help him not to escape his consequences, but to face them.

And yet, that's what she'd been afraid of when it came to her parents, that if she didn't toe the line, if she didn't want the same things they wanted, do what they wanted, then they would stop loving her. Worst of all, that was obviously exactly what they'd done.

And she'd survived. A wealth of strength rose up inside her as she thought of the past two years. She'd made it without them, and even though there had been times she'd longed for their support, she'd known deep in her heart that they were the ones lacking, not her.

"I was going to tell my parents about Nick," she finally said. "I was working up my nerve to tell them that he was the man I was going to be with, that he was the man who I loved, but before I got the chance to do that he was gone."

"And you never thought about how he might have felt through those months that you kept him a secret from everyone?" Lizzy asked.

Courtney took a sip of her coffee, stuffing back the

emotions that appeared out of nowhere at Lizzy's question. She cleared her throat, still stuffing as she thought of Nick's words before he'd left her the night before.

"I regret to say that I didn't. I was always just so deliriously happy whenever I was with him, so caught up in my own joy of believing he loved me that I never considered that he might think that I was keeping him a secret because I was somehow ashamed of him. It was fear that drove me, fear of my parents, but not any shame of Nick."

"But, Nick apparently doesn't know that." Lizzy took a big bite of the chocolate cake, chased it with a sip of coffee and then continued. "Courtney, I think you've been so caught up in your own bitterness you've been unable to look at the past from any other viewpoint."

Courtney leaned forward, remembering all the moments she and Nick had shared in the stall of the old barn. "When we were together we promised to love each other forever, to build a future together and have a family and live happily together forever. That's all I ever clung to when I left that barn and went back to my home in Evanston."

"And how much of that could he believe in when you left and went back to your 'real' life with your parents in Evanston? When you could only profess your love for him in the secrecy of that old, abandoned barn?"

Lizzy's words pierced Courtney's heart, not with her own pain but with what she imagined Nick must have felt each time she drove away from the Yates barn, each time she refused to be seen with him in public.

Now she remembered how many times he'd asked her to make their relationship open, how many times he'd told her that he wanted to share his love for her with the world, and each time she'd told him she needed more time before allowing that to happen.

"I wasn't even beside him on the day they buried his sister," Courtney said, tears pressing hot against her eyes. "Cherry's death devastated him, and while he buried his sister I was at a tea party my mother gave for all her little society friends."

Dear God. What had she done? She'd been so busy pointing the finger at him, she hadn't taken a minute to recognize her own culpability in what had ultimately happened between them.

"Don't look so sad," Lizzy said and reached out a hand to cover Courtney's. She squeezed her hand in comfort. "It sounds to me like what you and Nick both need to do is to sit down and talk about the past, really talk about it. You have to take some responsibility for not understanding his needs and wants when he did leave town."

She squeezed Courtney's hand again and then released it. "But I think the main thing you have to decide is what you really want from Nick. If you just want him in your life as a coparent to Garrett, then there's no reason to go back and pick at the past. You just go forward from here and leave the past alone. But, if you want something more from him then you're going to have to forget your own anger and bitterness and take on some of his."

Lizzy's words followed Courtney as she drove home. Night had fallen and Garrett was asleep in his car seat. Lizzy was right. She needed to talk to Nick and explain to him that it was fear that had driven her to keep him a secret, not shame…never shame.

It was also at that moment she realized that the moment she'd seen Nick again, deep in her heart, in her very soul, she'd wanted him back in her life, and not just as a coparent but as a friend and as a lover.

By the time she pulled up to her motel room, the parking lot was dark and quiet and she was exhausted. First thing in the morning she'd call Nick and make arrangements for them to talk…to really talk about what had happened between them.

She parked in the space outside her door and then grabbed her purse and got her sleeping son out of the car. He curled into her, deep in slumber, secure in his mother's arms.

She unlocked the door, flipped on the light and carried Garrett to his crib. She didn't bother to undress him, deciding that she'd give him a bath in the morning and dress him in his cutest outfit to see Nick.

Laying him down, she stood for a long moment next to the crib and gazed at him. As she looked at the little cleft in his chin, she knew that she'd never stop loving Nick. Just as he'd marked Garrett with that physical characteristic, he'd marked her heart forever.

The light went out, plunging the room into utter darkness.

"Damn," she muttered to herself, for the millionth time wishing she'd bought a lamp for the table next to her bed. Who knew how long that bulb had been burning in that light? Well, it wasn't burning now.

She made her way through the darkness to the bathroom, where she knew there was a package of new lightbulbs beneath the sink.

As she bent down to retrieve the bulbs, the bathroom door creaked closed behind her. For just a moment her heart stopped, and then she told herself that the motel was old, the floors uneven, and she laughed at her own jumpiness…until she tried to open the door.

It wouldn't budge. She yanked on the doorknob hard, and still the door didn't move. At the same time, she thought she heard movement coming from the room beyond the door, felt a malevolent energy that sent her heartbeat racing.

"Hey," she yelled as she dropped the lightbulb to the floor, where it bounced and rolled against the old linoleum. "Hey, who's out there?" She pulled on the doorknob, frantic to get out.

Panic scorched through her veins. Somebody was out there in the room with her son. No matter how hard she tried to open the door, she couldn't.

She screamed for help as she raced to the window and tried to pull it open, only to realize that at some point in time it had been painted closed. She grabbed a towel and quickly wrapped it around her arm, then slammed it against the window glass.

Rational thought was impossible. She was in a place where the only thing she needed was to get to her son. She had no idea what was happening, couldn't fathom why she couldn't open the bathroom door. She knew only the need to escape, to get out of the tiny room and to Garrett.

It took her three tries to finally smash through the bathroom window glass, and then she frantically crawled out, unmindful of the remaining shards that tore at her blouse and scratched her arms and legs as she slithered out the window and fell to the ground below.

She didn't waste time on the ground but sprang to her feet and raced for the side of the building. Tears blurred her vision, as she'd never known such fear as she did now. She turned the corner and ran for her motel room's front door.

As she opened the door, the red light from the nearby

neon sign spilled into the room and shone on the empty crib. With a new scream of anguish, Courtney fell to her knees.

Chapter 12

Nick had thought about Courtney and Garret all day long but had decided to give Courtney a little time to digest what had happened between them the night before.

He hadn't meant to say anything to her, hadn't wanted to rehash a past that was long gone, but the moment had presented itself and the emotions he'd kept suppressed for so long had finally slipped out of him.

He could tell he'd shocked her by what he'd said. The touch of bitterness in his voice as he'd spoken had surprised even him.

Still, he knew there was no way they could go forward in any kind of fashion until they'd somehow made peace with their past.

And he wanted to go forward. He had no idea in what capacity he would be in her life, but they had to go forward in some way so he could be an integral part of Garrett's life.

Even after just a day the absence of her and Garrett had put a hole in his heart, a hole he knew only they could fill. He knew it was possible he would never have Courtney in the way he wanted, in the way he needed her.

She'd already basically told him that he had no place in her life except as Garrett's father. But he kept thinking if he could somehow prove himself to her, if he could be the man she depended on, the one who loved her until the end of time, then maybe someday in the future they could find themselves together again as not just friends, but also as lovers and even more.

He'd been disappointed when he hadn't heard from her all day. Now it was after eleven and he should be in bed, but instead he remained on the sofa thinking about how past actions could poison future relationships.

He tamped down a touch of worry as he thought about the night of her car accident. There was no question that what she believed happened to her on that night worried him. If he'd had his way she would have never left here to go back to the motel.

What if she really did have a medical issue? What if she had something that caused blackouts? When he spoke to her again, he'd talk her into a full medical examination with the best doctors in Oklahoma. He didn't want to think about what might happen to her or to his son if that was the case.

His cell phone rang and he dug it out of his pocket, wondering who would be calling this late. When he saw Cameron Evans's name in the caller ID, his heart gave a sickening jump in his chest. "Sheriff?" he answered.

"Nick, I need you to come to the motel," Cameron said tersely.

"Why? What's going on?" Nick tried to tamp down

the sudden swell of anxiety that made him feel as if his breath had been halfway knocked out of him.

"Somebody was hiding in Courtney's room when she got home from having dinner with Lizzy Wiles in Rockville. Whoever it was locked her in the bathroom, and she had to break the window to get out."

"Is she all right?" Nick was already racing to the kitchen for his truck keys, his heart crashing against his ribs as he tried to process what Cameron was telling him.

"She'll be fine, but there's another problem."

Nick picked up the keys from the table and froze. "What other problem?"

"When she got out of the bathroom and ran back into the room, Garrett was gone. He's missing, Nick."

For a moment it was as if the world stopped spinning and the gravity had disappeared. Nick stumbled sideways, nearly falling to the floor as Cameron's words sank in.

"Nick…are you there?"

"I'm on my way."

Garrett gone? What did that mean? Nick rocketed out of the front door, got into his truck and started the engine with a roar.

Who would have attacked her? Who would want to take his son from her?

He gripped the steering wheel tightly, a fear he'd never known before racing through him. Where was Garrett? Where was his son?

Questions…so many questions and no answers. He felt as if he were being eaten from the inside out with the need to know now what had happened to Courtney and exactly where his son was at the moment.

A tight pressure threatened to cut off all the air to

his lungs as he stomped on the gas to get to the motel as quickly as possible. Who would want to take Garrett? His mind raced, but no real coherent thoughts could pierce through the gut-tightening terror that possessed him.

Maybe by the time he got there Cameron would tell him it had all been a mistake, that the bathroom door had stuck and Courtney had panicked, that Garrett had managed to crawl from his crib and had wandered outside only to be found hiding behind a nearby bush.

He wanted that. He needed everything to be all right. The idea of his son being anywhere else but in Courtney's or his own arms was positively unimaginable.

But as he pulled up into the motel entrance, he knew it wasn't a mistake and everything was dreadfully wrong. Not only was Cameron's car in front of Courtney's unit, but most of his deputies were also there.

As Nick stopped his truck and got out, he saw Courtney standing next to the sheriff. She trembled from head to toe, as if she were a fragile leaf in a wild windstorm.

When she saw him, her eyes opened wide and she ran to him, tears streaming down her cheeks as he opened his arms to catch her.

She threw her arms around his neck and sobbed uncontrollably as he held her tight against him. "He's gone, and I don't know what happened to him." She raised her head, her green eyes awash with pain...with fear.

"Somebody must have been hiding in my room. The light went out and I went to get a bulb and then the door wouldn't open and I crawled through the window and he was gone," she babbled, half-coherent as she cried.

"We'll find him," he assured her, although the sickness in his stomach nearly made him wretch. He looked at Cameron, hoping for a more complete story of exactly what had happened.

"From what we've been able to figure out, when Courtney got home somebody was already hiding in the room. When she placed Garrett in his crib, whoever was in the room unscrewed the lightbulb over the table and the room went black. Courtney went into the bathroom to get a new bulb, assuming it had burnt out, but when she got inside, the perp tied the bathroom door handle to the leg of the bed, making it impossible for Courtney to get out. We've dusted the lightbulb and around the table area, but found no fresh prints except Courtney's. I imagine whoever it was had on gloves."

He turned his attention back to Courtney. "Courtney, I've got my deputies going door-to-door to see if anyone saw anything, but I need both of you to come inside and answer some questions for me," Cameron said.

The last thing Nick wanted to do was go inside the motel room and waste time with questions he couldn't answer. What he wanted to do was rip the doors off every house in town, find the person who had his son and kill him for daring to put that look of terror in Courtney's eyes, for daring to hurt or take what was his.

As they entered the motel room, Nick stared in horror at the clothesline rope that had been used to lock Courtney in the bathroom.

Cameron saw the expression on his face. "Unfortunately, the rope is common. Half the people in Grady Gulch have a clothesline in their backyard, and it's sold everywhere."

He led them to the kitchen table, where the fingerprint dust had apparently been wiped off, although some of it still lingered in the cracks of the small table.

"I've got my deputies doing everything they can to

find Garrett," Cameron said once they were seated. "I need to know if either of you know of anyone who would have a reason to take Garrett."

Courtney leaned back weakly in the chair and shook her head. "No, I can't imagine. It doesn't make sense. This is all so crazy."

"The toys," Nick said suddenly. "You never figured out who left those toys."

Cameron frowned. "What toys?"

As Courtney explained to Cameron about the box of toys she'd found outside her room, Nick's thoughts were scattered to the wind by the fear that gripped his soul.

Surely this couldn't be a kidnapping for ransom. Although Nick was financially comfortable, he didn't have millions in the bank. So, if this hadn't been done for money, then why?

And was this connected to the toys that had been left for his son? The potential drugging that might have taken place on the night of Courtney's accident? Did it all tie together, or were they all just strange, isolated incidents?

Who could be behind all this? Had somebody drugged Courtney, hoping she'd have a fatal car accident so they could get access to Garrett?

He mentally shook his head. That didn't make sense. Even if Courtney was killed, whoever killed her would still have to know that they would have to contend with Nick.

"Where are these toys now?" Cameron asked when she'd finished explaining.

"I took them to the church. I felt weird about accepting them and I didn't want Garrett to have them."

Cameron made a note on his pad.

"What about Hubert?" Nick asked. Courtney looked

at him in surprise, but Nick continued. "The whole town knows he wasn't exactly thrilled when Courtney stopped seeing him. Maybe he's doing all this just to get back at her, to hurt her."

"Was he in the café the night of your accident?" Cameron asked.

Courtney nodded. "He was, although he didn't sit in my section."

"Still, he could have slipped something in her drink," Nick said.

"I'll check him out right now," Cameron replied, "but I've got to tell you, this doesn't feel like Grant's style. Still, an angry man can do things out of character."

Even though Cameron didn't look at Nick, he knew the lawman was thinking about Sam, who had gone off the deep end and done something completely out of character when he'd tried to kill Lizzy Wiles.

"I'd like you two to sit tight here while I coordinate my men and head to Grant's place. We'll find him, Courtney. I'll do everything in my power to find your son. Are you sure you can't think of anyone who might have shown an unusual interest in Garrett lately?"

Courtney shook her head. "No, other than the box of toys for him, there's been nothing...nobody."

"What about your parents?" Cameron asked.

It was obvious the question stunned her. "My parents?" She repeated the words as if they were speaking about aliens from another planet.

Cameron frowned. "I don't know all the history between you and your parents, but it's no secret that you're estranged from them. The new toys you told me about indicate some sort of caring for the boy. Maybe your parents decided it was finally time they meet their grandson."

Courtney's mouth opened and closed a couple of times, as if she were having trouble drawing breath. "And so they locked me in the bathroom and took my son?" Courtney asked incredulously as she shook her head. "Besides, I can't imagine them suddenly taking an interest in anything in my life, including my son. Still, if you think they need to be checked out, then do it."

"I'm definitely going to check them out," Cameron said. "I'm not leaving any stone unturned."

"Do whatever you need to do," Courtney said, a hint of steel in her voice. "Just bring me back our son."

"That's my plan," Cameron said. "I've called in all my men, and they're all out working the case. We'll find him." With these words he left the motel room.

Once he was gone, tears once again started to trek down Courtney's cheeks.

They both placed their cell phones on the table and then Nick reached out for her hand and she clutched at his as if it were her only lifeline.

He felt the same way, that her touch kept him grounded, saved him from going completely out of his mind with fear.

For several long minutes they didn't speak, but squeezed hands tightly as a wail of fear remained silent but evident in the air between them.

"I'm so sorry…" she began.

"Stop, there's nothing for you to be sorry about," he replied. "You couldn't have known that somebody somehow managed to get into your room and lock you in the bathroom to take Garrett. This isn't your fault, Courtney."

She nodded. "I know, but I'm also sorry about the past. I just want you to know that you were never a dirty little secret to me, that it was fear of my parents rather than any shame of being seen with you that made me keep everything about you a secret. I'm sorry, Nick. I'm so sorry about everything that happened in the past."

Although her words pierced through the shell of anger that had lightly coated his heart, he couldn't think about the past right now. All he could focus on at the moment was his missing son. Garrett. Where was Garrett?

"We can talk about all that later," he said. "What we need to do right now is try to figure out who is behind all this and why, and where somebody has taken our son."

Courtney released her grip on his hand and instead rubbed her hand across her forehead as if in an attempt to ease a headache. "I just can't begin to imagine."

"Did you get checked out by a doctor?" Nick asked as he noticed the cuts and scratches on her arms.

"I'm fine. Everything is mostly superficial," she assured him. Her eyes once again filled with tears. "I just need my baby back."

She slapped a hand down onto the top of the table in sudden anger. "I should be out there looking for him, not sitting here helplessly."

"Cameron is good at what he does. We have to trust him and his team to do their jobs. Besides, if the toys and this kidnapping are tied together, then my hope is that whoever has Garrett has no intention to harm him," Nick said. He just prayed he was right, for the alternative was too horrible to imagine.

Courtney toggled between tears and a strange numbness as her fear peaked with every minute that passed. The darkness outside was profound, and Garrett should be in his little cowboy pajamas and asleep in his crib. The world wasn't right, and it would never be right until she had Garrett back in her arms once again.

The silence of the cell phones in the center of the table only added to her overall anxiety. Why didn't somebody call? If it was a kidnapping for ransom, then why didn't somebody call and make their demands? Whatever the amount, she would figure out a way to pay it. Together she and Nick would give them whatever they wanted as long as they got Garrett back safe and sound.

Why, oh why didn't somebody just call to tell them Garrett had been found and the world had been made right again. Her head felt as if it were about to explode as she tried to think of who could be behind this, who might want to take her baby boy.

"Rusty." The name exploded from her lips.

Nick frowned at her. "Rusty Albright. Why would the cook at the Cowboy Café have anything to do with this?"

"I just know that the other day Rusty was in a really bad mood and Mary confided in me that years ago he'd lost his wife and child in a house fire. The baby boy was about Garrett's age when the fire happened. It was like the ten-year anniversary, and he was really upset. He always asks about Garrett…" Her voice trailed off.

Was it possible that something had snapped inside Rusty? That somehow the past had exploded in his brain and he'd decided that Garrett was the little boy he'd lost.

She watched as Nick grabbed his cell phone. He punched in a number. "Mary, it's Nick. Is Rusty working tonight?" Courtney watched every muscle in Nick's body tense. "Okay, thanks." He slid his phone closed, his eyes dark. "Rusty isn't working."

Courtney got up from the table. "Then let's go find him."

Even though Cameron had told them to sit tight, she knew Nick was with her as he rose from the table and shoved his phone into his pocket.

She grabbed hers as well, and within seconds they were in his truck and roaring out of the motel parking lot. For the first time since she'd seen the empty crib, a tiny ray of hope flittered through her heart.

She knew Rusty. He had a reputation for being a tough loner who didn't take any crap from anyone, but surely he wouldn't hurt a child. If he had somehow snapped because of the trauma of his past and he'd taken Garrett in a delusional state, believing Garrett was his son, then she would be able to forgive him as long as he got some sort of psychiatric help.

"It has to be him," she said aloud. "He always asks about Garrett. He would have had access to my drink. He could have dropped that box of toys off at the motel, and he probably knows how to pick a lock on a door. Maybe his sense of reality cracked."

"I don't give a damn what cracked. If he's got my kid, he's got a problem," Nick replied tersely.

"Maybe we should call Cameron and tell him where we're going?" she suggested.

"No. I want to check this out myself. We'll go to Rusty's cabin, and if he isn't there then we'll call in Cameron." Nick stepped on the gas and a sense of urgency filled Courtney as they drew closer to the Cowboy Café and the four cabins behind it, including one where Rusty lived.

Courtney's heart thundered in her chest, like a frantic drum that resonated through her entire body. She told herself this had to be right, that they were going to get to Rusty's cabin and find Garrett there safe and sound. There would be no ugly confrontation, the sight of them would snap Rusty out of whatever mental delusion he'd suffered, and he'd be apologetic and horrified by what he'd done.

The tiny ray of hope exploded into a shining ball as Nick reached the parking lot of the café and headed around to the back of the building, where the four small cabins were located.

Three of them had been left empty after Candy Bailey, the first waitress, had been murdered in hers. Cameron had moved out the other single women but had agreed to allow Rusty to continue living in the one on the far end.

Hope soared through her as she saw a light shining from Rusty's cabin and his beat-up red pickup truck parked outside. "He's here," she said, her heart beating so fast she was breathless.

As Nick came to a stop in front of the cabin, Courtney prayed that Garrett was inside, happily playing with toys Rusty had bought for him. She needed to have Garrett in her arms right now. She couldn't wait another minute.

When Nick's truck came to a stop, they both jumped out. Nick beat her to the door, banging on it with the force of a jackhammer.

"Hold your damn horses," Rusty's deep voice yelled from inside. He jerked open his door and took a step back at the sight of them. "Nick…Courtney…what's up?"

It was obvious Rusty had been relaxing. He wore an old worn T-shirt and cutoff denim shorts that showcased legs the size of tree trunks.

"You got our boy?" Nick asked, the tension taut in his voice.

Rusty frowned. "What the hell are you talking about?" He looked from Nick to Courtney, genuine confusion in his blue eyes. "Courtney? What's going on?"

It was at that moment Courtney knew her baby wasn't here. Where was Garrett? She turned to Nick and burst into tears.

Chapter 13

Minutes later they were back in Nick's truck, but still parked in front of Rusty's cabin. "I was so sure," she cried. "I was so sure this was the answer."

Rusty had fully cooperated when Nick had asked to come in and look around, and both he and Courtney were satisfied that Rusty had nothing to do with the missing little boy.

"At least this made some sort of sense," Nick replied. He hadn't even started his truck. It was as if he didn't know what to do next, where to go.

She felt the same way...lost in a miasma of emotions that felt far too close to grief. And she didn't want to feel grief. That implied she had lost something precious, and Garrett wasn't lost forever—he was merely temporarily misplaced.

"I just can't imagine anyone else who might have done this," she finally said as her burst of tears ebbed.

"We'd better head back to the motel and wait to see what Cameron and his deputies have found," Nick said as he started the truck.

"If they had found something somebody would have called us," she replied, fighting against an overwhelming despair.

She stared out the window, the darkness outside a misery in her soul. Who would want to do this? Who would want to hurt her? Hurt Nick? Who would want to take away their precious son?

They both jumped in their seats as Nick's cell phone rang. He pulled to the side of the road and fumbled with one hand to get it out of his pocket and answer.

She sat forward in her seat as far as the seat belt would allow. She could tell by his expression that it wasn't good news, nor was it bad. Nick listened for a moment, then said goodbye and clicked off the phone.

"That was Cameron. He was at your parents' house, where they were in the middle of a dinner party. There was no indication that they had anything to do with Garrett's disappearance."

Courtney nodded, a faint edge of sadness momentarily stealing her abject fear for her son. "They haven't wanted anything to do with him or me for the last two years, so I couldn't imagine that they'd suddenly gotten a desire to kidnap Garrett."

"He also told me that Ben Temple checked out Grant, who was at The Corral with a couple of buddies and had been there for the past several hours." He slammed his hand down on the steering wheel. "That puts us back to square one," he said in obvious frustration. "The suspects we had, Grant, Rusty and your parents, are all off the list of suspects." His voice deepened with each word and his eyes darkened to a blue she'd never seen before. "So, who has our son?" he asked hoarsely. "I've only had him for a little over a week. Why would somebody take him away from me? From us?"

Courtney's heart ached not only with her own pain but also with his. She reached across the seat and placed her hand on his, as if only by connecting could they find the strength to get through all of this.

"Cameron is on his way back to the motel," Nick said as he once again put the truck in drive and merged back onto the road.

Once again she stared out the passenger window, where the darkness felt like an enemy who had swallowed her son and now refused to let him go.

Garrett was out there, Courtney thought in despair. She desperately hoped Nick was right, that somehow the toys and the kidnapping were connected and whoever had taken Garrett had tucked him gently into a nicely covered crib.

She desperately hoped Garrett wasn't afraid. The mental vision of him standing in a crib, crying out for her, sickened her and brought a new veil of tears to her eyes.

As Nick pulled back into the motel parking lot, Courtney fought against the scream of torment that worked its way up the back of her throat.

"Go to the office," she said. Nick gave her a quick, curious look, and she shrugged. "Maybe Mickey has remembered something since Cameron spoke to him earlier."

Nick nodded and pulled in front of the motel office. Courtney knew he felt what she did, the need to do something even if it had already been done.

Mickey Jeffries was a thirty-year-old who worked the desk at the motel from seven in the evening until seven in the morning. He was an affable young man whose bright smile mitigated the fact that he had ears to rival a baby elephant's.

His smile was nowhere in sight as Nick and Courtney walked into the small office that smelled of burned coffee and freshly baked cookies. "Any news?" he asked as he stood from his chair behind the desk.

Courtney shook her head. "We were just wondering if you'd thought of anything else since Cameron spoke to you." As she waited for him to answer, she wondered how long her heart could continue the frantic beat in her chest, how long could she remain in this horrendous state of limbo?

"No. I mean, Sheriff Evans asked me if I'd seen anyone around your room throughout the evening, but I didn't pay any attention. I usually just sit behind the desk until somebody comes in, and tonight was pretty quiet."

Courtney knew it had been a long shot. "Thanks, Mickey." She began to turn to leave, but her attention was caught by the plate of cookies that sat on the counter. They were artfully arranged on a red paper plate with a pink doily.

She froze. Where had she seen that before? "Those look nice and fresh," she said, racking her brain to remember where she'd seen cookies arranged like that before.

"Yeah, the last couple of weeks Abigail Swisher has been coming by and dropping off cookies for the staff and guests. She bakes a mean chocolate chip cookie." He looked stricken. "Jeez, I didn't mention to Sheriff Evans that she'd dropped by earlier."

Abigail. Of course, she'd brought a plate of cookies to Courtney while she'd been in the hospital. As Courtney and Nick left the office, Courtney's brain flashed with thoughts and images.

Abigail…who had lost a baby about the same time that Garrett had been born. Abigail, who often came to the park at the same time Courtney took Garrett. Abigail had been in the café the night that Courtney thought she'd been drugged.

The last thing Courtney wanted to do was point a finger at an innocent woman, but the more she thought about it, the more she wondered about Abigail.

Had she had some sort of psychotic snap? Had she somehow fell into a delusion where she thought Garrett was her son? That's what you thought about Rusty, she reminded herself, and you were wrong about him.

Still, she couldn't get the thought out of her head. As she and Nick stepped back out into the darkness of night, she couldn't hold it in any longer. "Nick?"

He turned to look at her, his features taut with tension, but softening slightly as he gazed at her. "Yeah?"

"I think maybe we need to talk to Abigail Swisher."

He frowned. "Abigail? Why her?"

The more Courtney thought about it, the more frantically her heart beat. She told him everything that was whirling around in her mind. "Am I crazy, or is it possible?"

"If you're crazy then I'm right there with you. Let's go," he said, immediately pulling her back to his truck.

"Maybe we should call Cameron? He'll wonder where we've gone."

"We'll call when we get closer to the Swisher place," Nick replied.

Minutes later they were on their way to Abigail's farmhouse. Nick had called Cameron, who was still on his way back from Evanston and wasn't happy with them, but Cameron's disapproval of them going out alone didn't slow Nick's speed.

"I don't want you talking to her," Courtney said. She held up a hand to still the protest she knew Nick would make. "If what I think is true, then she's sick and I don't want you coming at her. I'll approach her woman to woman, see if I can get inside the house and see any indication that Garrett is there. You already went at Rusty like you were going to tear his head off, and we were wrong."

"If we'd been right I would have torn his head off," Nick replied darkly.

"I need to go in first, Nick. It's a gut instinct, a woman's intuition," she said.

"I don't like it," Nick replied flatly.

"It's the way we need to do it, Nick. I feel it in my heart. I need to approach her softly. You can be right outside and can come in if necessary. But, if she's an innocent woman and my instincts are all wrong, I don't want her upset."

"Surely Fred wouldn't have anything to do with something like kidnapping a kid," Nick said.

"The last few times I've seen her, she's mentioned that Fred is out of town." Courtney thought of Abigail's husband, a soft-spoken man who wore a veil of sadness about him.

Nick's frown was evident in the illumination from the dashboard. "But, this still doesn't make sense. How on earth would Abigail think she could keep Garrett in this small town and nobody would know? The minute she bought a box of diapers somebody would question it, since she doesn't have any kids."

"I don't know," Courtney replied. "It doesn't make sense, and that's why it's possible this is just another wild goose chase. Abigail is a nice woman who suffered a terrible tragedy. I wouldn't want to accuse her of something she isn't guilty of."

Courtney's heart banged painfully hard as Nick pulled into the Swisher drive. The long drive led to a small ranch house. "I don't see Fred's pickup," Nick said.

"And I don't see Abigail's SUV," Courtney said, wondering if it was possible nobody was home. Was it Abigail who had been hiding in the park that day, watching Courtney and Nick as they'd played with Garrett? Was it possible the woman had dropped something in Courtney's drink in an effort to harm her?

Had that been the beginning of some bizarre plan to steal Garrett away from Courtney? It sounded positively crazy, especially given Nick's presence in town, in their lives.

"Maybe nobody is home," she said as they drew closer.

"It's lit up like somebody is home," Nick replied.

He parked in front of the house, unfastened his seat belt and turned to her. "Are you sure you want to go up there alone?"

"Positive," she said despite the nerves that screamed just beneath the surface of her skin.

"Unfortunately, you aren't the boss in this particular situation," he replied. "I'll let you go to the door and talk to her, but I'm going to be right off the porch where she can't see me, close enough that if you get into trouble I'll be right there."

"Okay, but I'm not expecting any trouble. Still, if there is trouble, trust me, I know how to scream." Courtney stared at the house and thought she saw a shadow move behind the curtains at the front window. "Somebody's home," she muttered.

Drawing a deep breath, she got out of the truck and didn't even look to see if Nick followed. She was focused solely on the idea that there was a possibility that her son was inside, that he needed to be back where he belonged...with her and Nick.

This thought forced a surge of strength inside her. If Garrett was inside, then she wouldn't let anything or anyone stop her from getting to him.

As she walked toward the front door, she was aware of Nick blending into the shadows of the night and moving to stand just out of sight next to the front porch.

This was probably a waste of time, she thought as she stopped at the front door. Abigail had always seemed so nice, so normal. Courtney raised her hand to knock, but hesitated a moment. Was she mentally stringing together a series of events to Abigail in a desperate effort to find her son? There was only one way to find out. She rapped on the door and tensed as she heard footsteps approaching from the other side.

The door opened and Abigail greeted her with a startled look. "Courtney, what a surprise," she said. "Can I help you with something? It's a bit late for a social visit, isn't it?" Abigail held the door tight in her hands only halfway open. But, in the space of the open door Courtney saw a couple of suitcases sitting just inside the door.

"Oh, are you going somewhere?" Courtney asked, trying to keep her tone light and friendly even though she wanted to storm through the door and search the house for her son.

"I told you the other day that Fred was on a business trip, but the truth is he's in Dallas with his parents. We had a little spat about a month ago that kind of spiraled out of control, but everything is going to be all right now and I'm going down to his parents' house to meet him."

Abigail beamed at Courtney, and then her smile fell into a frown of confusion. "But, you never said why you're here."

At that moment a faint cry came from someplace behind Abigail. It wasn't just any cry. It was the sound of an unhappy little boy...Courtney's unhappy little boy.

"I've got to go now," Abigail said, but as she tried to close the door Courtney stuck her foot in it so that Abigail couldn't shut her out.

"Who's that? Who is that crying?" she asked. Her heart beat loudly in her ears as Garrett's cries grew louder.

Abigail smiled, and in the hazy glow of that smile Courtney realized the woman had lost all touch with reality. "That's my boy, Jason. You haven't met him. He's been sickly for a while, so I don't take him out much."

"Since I'm here, could I meet him now?" Courtney wondered just how distant Abigail was from the real world. "You know, I have a little boy, too."

"Oh, yes, I know. Sweet little Garrett. Jason is just about his age."

"So, can I meet your Jason?" Courtney felt as if she was about to explode. There was no question that the child in the house was Garrett, and thankfully there was no reason to believe that he was in any real danger.

But it was obvious Abigail had suffered some sort of delusional snap, and that meant there was no way to second-guess what she might be capable of.

"I guess it wouldn't hurt for you to meet my Jason," Abigail said. She opened the door wider to allow Courtney into the neat living room. As she closed the door behind them, Courtney wondered where Nick was and if he'd heard any of their conversation. Had he heard Garrett's faint cry?

She followed Abigail down a hallway, her heart beating so fast she felt as if she might be on the verge of a heart attack. She drew a couple of deep breaths to steady herself. Garrett had stopped crying, but she could hear his little voice gibbering softly as they approached the first doorway.

"He's a good boy, and of course he's missed his daddy since Fred has been gone. But, both Fred and I agree that it's important that a child grows up in an intact family."

Abigail ushered Courtney into a bedroom that had been set up as a nursery complete with teddy bear curtains and wallpaper border, a rocking chair and a crib. And in the crib Garrett pulled himself up as they entered, and his eyes lit with happiness as he held his arms out to Courtney. "Mama!"

Courtney's knees nearly sagged in relief to see him not only healthy but also obviously not tremendously traumatized as he leaned down and picked up a plastic book. "Toy," he said. She fought the impulse to run to him, to grab him up in her arms and flee out the door.

Poor Abigail. She needed help. Courtney had no idea what had happened between Abigail and Fred, but it was easy to guess that when Fred left, Abigail had snapped.

She turned to look at the woman and gasped as she saw that "poor Abigail" held a large butcher knife in her hand and blocked the door of the bedroom.

"You can't have him back," she said as she advanced a couple of steps toward Courtney. "He's mine now. He's going to make everything all right between me and Fred. When I lost my baby, they told me I couldn't have any more. Even though Fred told me it didn't matter, it did. But, now I can give him Jason, and we can be a family."

Courtney could hardly tear her gaze off the knife. "But, Abigail, he's not yours. He's mine." Where was Nick? As Courtney looked into the depths of Abigail's brown eyes, she realized she was in trouble, that there was no way Abigail intended for her to leave the bedroom with Garrett.

"He needs Fred and me, not you. You're just a single woman trying to raise him on a waitress's tips. He deserves more than that." Abigail took another step toward her, and Courtney's heart leaped into her throat.

"You left the toys for him, didn't you?" she asked.

"They were good toys, the kind he deserves to have. My Jason deserves the best. He deserves nice toys and two parents."

"He has two parents," Courtney protested, stepping backward and away from the crib, but aware that she was slowly backing herself into a corner. "He has me and he has Nick."

Abigail's smile held no humor. "Nick Benson? What kind of a father could he be? Here one minute, gone the next. If you would have died in that car accident, it would have made everything much easier. You shouldn't have come here tonight. If you would have waited another thirty minutes, I would have been gone and you wouldn't have had to die. Now you know I can't let you leave here alive."

Fear shuddered through Courtney as Garrett stood up in the crib once again and called to her. She didn't look at her son. She didn't want to take her gaze off the woman who held the wicked knife and was coming closer…closer still.

"Even if you kill me, Nick will never let you have Garrett."

"His name is Jason, and trust me, the last thing Nick

Benson will want is to be saddled with a kid and try to be a single father. He's got enough on his plate with his boozed-up brother and the other one in jail."

The scary part to Courtney was that she could tell that Abigail believed everything she was saying. She thought that all she had to do was kill Courtney and then Nick would agree to let her take Garrett and she'd go try to reconcile with her husband.

Where was Nick? Courtney didn't want to scream. She didn't want to traumatize Garrett. Frantically she looked around, seeking something she could use as a weapon, something that might provide some kind of self-defense against the knife. But, there was nothing, nothing that stood between herself and a desperate, crazy woman with a knife.

Chapter 14

Nick fought against an edge of panic when the two women disappeared into the house. He wasn't sure whether to barge into the front door or somehow try to figure out exactly where in the house they had gone.

He finally decided to circle the house and peek into the windows and see if he could get a handle on Courtney's location. He wasn't sure if Garrett was inside, he wasn't sure if Courtney was in trouble or not, but he was comforted slightly by the fact that the bit of conversation he'd initially heard had sounded friendly and so far there had been no screams or panicked cries coming from within.

Unfortunately, his trek around the house told him nothing. All the shades were pulled down tight, not allowing him even a little peek inside.

When he could stand it no longer, he returned to the front of the house and grabbed the doorknob, breathing a sigh of relief as it turned and the door eased open. There was no sign of either Abigail or Courtney, but he heard Abigail's voice coming from someplace down the hallway. And what he heard chilled him to the bone.

He raced down the hall and turned into the first bedroom. In an instant his brain absorbed what was before him. Garrett stood in a crib, and Abigail was advancing on Courtney, who stood in the corner, her green eyes nearly black with terror.

"Abigail!" He yelled her name, and when she whirled around he saw the knife she held in her hand.

"You can't have him," she shrieked as she raced toward him, the knife raised high for attack. He instinctively raised his hands in front of him in defense, shocked when the knife sliced through his forearm.

As she attacked again, slashing the knife with homicidal intent, he dodged the weapon and tried to grab her wrist. Abigail wasn't a big woman, but she was a woman driven by desperation and adrenaline.

He finally managed to grab the wrist that held the knife, but she twisted out of his grip, and he groaned in surprise as he felt the knife pierce through his chest.

He was vaguely aware of Courtney running to the crib and pulling Garrett into her arms even as Abigail moved to cut him again.

Someplace in the back of his mind he knew the wound on his chest was fairly deep and bleeding badly. He couldn't let her win. This was about his woman and his child. He couldn't allow a crazy woman to harm the two people he loved more than anyone or anything else.

With a roar of rage, and using the last of his strength, he tackled Abigail to the floor, grappling for the knife. Abigail screamed in outrage as he finally managed to pin her arm to the floor.

"He's mine," she cried. "I deserve to have him. He's my Jason."

"He's my son," Nick said with a low growl of anger. "And his name is Garrett." Nick had never hit a woman in his life, but as Abigail continued to fight him, struggling to get her arm free to attack again, Nick slammed his fist into her jaw.

She grunted as if in surprise and then slumped unmoving on the floor. At that moment Cameron Evans flew through the door, his eyes wild as he took in the scene before him.

Nick got up from the floor slowly, feeling a bit lightheaded as he offered a weak smile to the sheriff. "I guess we went off like the lone rangers, but we managed to get the job done." He smiled at Courtney, who gave him a tremulous, tear-filled smile back.

"Mama," Garrett said and then pointed at Nick. "Dada."

Nick's heart swelled so full in his chest he couldn't breathe. Dada. Garrett had called him Dada. The lightheadedness slammed into him, and he felt himself falling. He knew he was going to lose consciousness, but it was okay. Courtney and Garrett were safe, Cameron was here and all was right with the world.

Courtney sat next to the hospital bed, her fingers worrying a stray thread on the bottom of her blouse. It had been an endless night. Even though they'd managed to save Garrett, when Nick collapsed on the floor, Courtney had nearly fallen down herself.

He'd been bleeding from nicks and a large slash wound on his arm, but it was the cut on his chest that had scared her to death as she wondered what kind of damage had been done.

After that, things became blurred in her head. An ambulance had arrived to whisk Nick away, Abigail was taken into custody and Garrett had cried and fussed as if aware of his mother's emotional stress.

Cameron had left his men in charge to begin gathering evidence while he drove her and Garrett to the hospital. By the time they arrived there, Lizzy and Daniel had heard the news and had shown up. Lizzy offered to take the sleepy Garrett home with them and Courtney, trusting her friend with her life, agreed.

Now that she knew Garrett was safe and Abigail was in jail, all her thoughts were on Nick, who had been taken into the emergency room for treatment.

The next hour seemed to last a lifetime as she'd awaited word on his condition. She still couldn't quite comprehend what had happened, the fact that Abigail had been behind it all, that she'd wanted Garrett to replace the baby she'd lost.

Finally, Dr. Spiro had come out to let her know that Nick had required thirteen stitches in his arm and that the knife wound to the chest had nicked one of his lungs.

The doctor believed the nick was small enough that it would heal on its own, so he was nixing the idea of surgery. Still, he'd given Nick a sedative to make him rest through the night and indicated that he would be watched carefully for any change to his condition.

Courtney now got up from the chair and moved to the hospital window, where the sun had finally made an appearance, announcing the end of the long, horrible night.

She stretched with arms overhead and then returned to her chair and gazed at Nick. His thick, dark hair was mussed, and she fought the impulse to gently move an errant strand off his forehead. His features were relaxed, his mouth slightly open, and she wanted to cover those lips with her own.

He was her father's son, but he was also the man of her heart. No matter what had happened in the past, he'd put himself in front of a knife-wielding crazy woman to save his son because that was the kind of man he was, because that was the kind of father he'd be.

His eyelids fluttered several times and then she was looking into the beautiful blue depths of his gaze. He gave her a slightly loopy, crooked smile. "What happened?"

"You're a hero. You're *my* hero. Unfortunately at the moment, you're a slightly damaged one. Thirteen stitches on the arm, a couple on your chest, a punctured lung and various nicks and scratches."

"Will I live?" he asked in a light, still slightly slurred voice.

"Definitely." She leaned forward and placed a hand on his shoulder, needing to touch him. "But, you've certainly given me a long night."

"Where's Garrett?"

"With Daniel and Lizzy. I didn't want him here, but I didn't want to leave your side until I saw those baby blues of yours."

"He called me dada…or did I dream that?" he asked.

"He definitely called you dada," she replied.

He closed his eyes, as if savoring this information, then opened his eyes again, shifted positions and winced slightly. "How long am I in for?"

"At least the rest of today and tonight, and then the doctor will check about letting you go home tomorrow, but I wouldn't count on it."

"I'd like to get out of here now," he replied, his voice

still thick with the sedatives and painkillers he'd been given throughout the night.

She smiled. "That's not happening, cowboy."

"And you're the boss, right?"

"That's right." Her smile faltered as tears pressed at her eyes and blurred her vision. "Oh, Nick, I was so afraid. When you were fighting with Abigail, I was so terrified for you."

"I wasn't about to let that knife-wielding nutcase get the better of me." He took her hand in his, and as always she felt the simple connection deep inside her heart. "I protect what is mine."

A wealth of emotion pressed tight against her chest. "Thank you, Nick, for being a great father…for being the kind of man I'd want as a father to my son." She stared at their entwined hands. "I wronged you in the past. I wasn't the kind of woman you needed, and for that I'll always be sorry. I wish I could go back and do those seven months all over again. I wish I would have confronted my parents, that I would have been standing next to you on the day that you buried your sister." She looked at him and realized he was once again asleep. She had no idea if he'd heard what she'd said to him or not.

Realizing he'd probably be out for some time, she got up from the chair, leaned over and kissed him softly on the forehead and left the room.

Nick remained in the hospital for five days, the doctor insisting he stay in bed until the nick in the lung was well into the healing process.

Courtney and Garrett visited him every day, keeping the conversation light and entertaining as he got grouchy about what he considered a long confinement. The food made him cranky, and he complained that he couldn't get any sleep and all he wanted to do was go home.

Courtney had taken a leave of absence from her job waitressing at the café with Mary's blessing. Courtney's sole focus for the past week had been Garrett and Nick.

Cameron had been in and out, tying up loose ends regarding Abigail Swisher. According to Cameron, Fred and Abigail's marriage had fallen completely apart about a month before she'd kidnapped Garrett. Fred had known nothing about what Abigail had been doing since the time he'd left town. At that time the room that was now a nursery in their home had simply been a spare bedroom.

Cameron had no reason to believe that Fred had been involved in any way in Abigail's plans, and she was being held in jail pending a psychiatric evaluation.

Adam had returned from his trip to visit his friends looking both rested and mentally stronger. He instantly bonded with Garrett, and vowed to Nick that he was determined to get back to the land of the living.

It had warmed Courtney's heart to see the relationship beginning to rebuild between the two brothers. She knew Nick wanted that and believed that Adam needed it.

What she didn't know exactly was where she and Nick stood with their relationship. She knew he loved her and she was as deeply in love with him as she'd been years ago. But, she felt as if there was still some unfinished business between them, and she wasn't sure how to go about fixing it.

She didn't realize what it was until the morning she came to pick him up from the hospital. She'd left Garrett with Sophie for the morning so she could do what she felt needed to be done.

As she walked into the hospital room, he was up and dressed in a pair of tight jeans and a clean white T-shirt, and his cowboy hat sat on the edge of the bed.

Courtney wore a mint-colored sundress that she knew enhanced her green eyes and dark hair. She was nervous as she felt as if today was the day her future would be determined. She would either be with Nick for the rest of her life or he would remain a part-time babydaddy and nothing more.

"Am I glad to see you," he greeted her. "And you look positively gorgeous."

She grinned. "You'd think I was gorgeous if I had a paper bag over my head and was dressed in a burlap sack, because you know I'm here to spring you from this place."

"I've been ready to get out of here for the last two days, and I'd think you looked beautiful even if you were wearing a burlap bag and didn't have the keys to your car in hand." He picked up his hat from the bed. "My paperwork is all in order, so I'm ready to go."

"How are you feeling?" she asked as they headed down the long hallway that would lead them to the exit.

"Good, ready to get back to real life."

"You feel like going on a little drive?" she asked.

He looked at her in surprise. "A drive?"

She nodded. "It's something I need to do, and I'd like you to be with me."

"Okay," he said slowly as they stepped out into the morning heat. "Are you going to be any less cryptic about it?"

She flashed him a smile. "I don't think so." She opened the driver door of her rental car. "Consider your-self in my custody for about the next hour."

"Hmm, I like the sound of that," he replied and got into the passenger seat.

Courtney started the car and headed out of the hospital parking lot and immediately got on the highway that would lead them out of Grady Gulch and toward Evanston.

She tried to ignore the beat of her heart, which quickened with every mile she drove. Nick cast her several curious glances, but he didn't ask any questions about their destination.

"Are you going to let me take you and Garrett to the town festival next week?" he asked.

"We'd love to go with you," she replied. Strange how much things had changed in the past couple of weeks. The last time she'd thought about the town festival, she'd been making plans to attend with Grant.

"We'll make a whole day of it," he said. "I can't wait to introduce Garrett to cotton candy and funnel cake."

"And then you get to clean him up after he throws up from too many sweets," she replied.

He flashed her that lazy, sexy smile of his. "I figure if I learned to diaper one end I can figure out how to clean the other end."

She laughed and realized that no matter what happened in the next fifteen minutes, she would always love Nick Benson as she'd love no other man.

It wasn't until she turned on the street where her parents lived that Nick spoke again. "Courtney, you know you don't have to do this," he said softly.

"I know."

"Are you even sure you know what you're doing?" he asked, worry in his voice.

"Maybe…maybe not, but it's something I want to do, something I have to do." She pulled up into the driveway of a huge, brick, two-story colonial and cut the engine. She unbuckled her seat belt and turned to look at him.

"Nick, I can't go back and make the past right. I can't fix what's already done. At that time I was an immature fool who couldn't see beyond my own issues, my own needs." Pressure built up in her chest… A depth of emotion that had nothing to do with herself and everything to do with him.

"I know this is probably too little, too late, but it's something I have to do for me…for us." She glanced toward the house where she'd lived for twenty-four years, and a knot of anxiety tightened in the center of her stomach.

Now that she thought about it, it was a familiar knot of tension, one that had always been with her when she'd been living in that house with her parents.

"Would you go with me to the front door?" she asked.

His gaze held hers, and in his eyes she found not only an acceptance of the past, but the faint glimmer of hope for the future. "I'll be right beside you," he said.

Despite the frantic, nervous butterflies that took flight in her stomach as she got out of the car, she was also armed with a sense of rightness.

She'd slunk away from here as a disgraced, tossed-away, disobedient child, and she was returning as a strong, vibrant woman who knew exactly what she wanted from life.

As they headed for the front door, Nick caught her hand in his, as if in an attempt to offer her whatever support she needed. But, the closer they got to the door the less the butterflies flew in her stomach and instead a rise of indignation, of anger, replaced them.

She dropped Nick's hand to knock on the door. A moment later her mother, Connie, opened it and stared in stunned surprise. "Courtney." She said the name without inflection, making it impossible for Courtney to know if she was happy or sad to see her.

"Hello, Mother," Courtney replied. As usual her mother was dressed in a conservative light pink suit, as if she were on her way to one of her many club meetings or social events.

"What are you doing here?" Connie asked.

"I just wanted to stop by and introduce you to Nick Benson." She grabbed Nick's arm possessively. "He's the man I was seeing two years ago, the man who fathered Garrett, my son."

Nick tipped his hat and Courtney continued. "As you can see, Nick is a cowboy. He's part owner of a ranch in Grady Gulch, and he's the only man I've ever loved. I'm hoping to build a life with him, and if that life includes mucking manure from horse stalls, I'm all in. We won't be throwing any fancy parties, but we might have a few barbecues for friends and neighbors, and I'll probably spill barbecue sauce down my chin and onto whatever blouse I'm wearing."

Courtney's mother shook her head, a touch of sadness coupled with disdain on her elegant features. "Oh, Courtney, we groomed you for so much better."

"Groomed me?" Courtney released a slightly bitter laugh. "I was your daughter, Mother, not a dog to be groomed and trained."

Connie's nostrils thinned. "So, why are you here now?"

"I just wanted to let you know that I'm happy and that I'm choosing love over anything else in my life. I wanted you to know that my love comes with a cowboy hat instead of a three-piece suit, and I'd hoped that you'd be happy for me."

"You've been nothing but a disappointment to your father and me," Connie replied.

Courtney raised her chin, expecting nothing less from the people who had raised her. "And may I just say, the feeling is mutual."

She was equally unsurprised when her mother stepped back and closed the door with the audible sound of a lock falling into place.

"Wow," Nick said as he placed an arm around Courtney. "Are you okay?"

She smiled up at him. "I'm better than okay."

"That was pretty tough."

"It was nothing more than what I expected." She released a tremulous sigh. "I was never a daughter to them. I was always just a project, like my dad working on the mayor's Christmas tree or my mother's charity events. All they ever wanted from me was to be a positive reflection on them, on their social standing in their community. I was never a daughter to be loved and cherished, to be nurtured to make my own choices and find my own happiness."

Nick placed his arms around her waist and pulled her close. "You didn't have to do this for me, Courtney."

"No, I needed to do it for me," she replied. "And I somehow felt that we couldn't move on until I did it. And I want to move on, Nick. I want a life with you and Garrett together as a family."

"And you meant what you said about mucking out stalls?" One of his dark eyebrows quirked upward in obvious amusement.

"Okay, I might have exaggerated that part a little bit," she admitted.

"You know what I want to do right now?" he asked.

"What's that?"

His lazy grin dropped away and his eyes deepened in a way that sent a delicious chill up her spine. "I want to kiss you right here, right on your parents' front porch."

"I say go for it, cowboy," she replied tremulously.

"And you're the boss, right?" he asked teasingly.

"Darned right," she managed to mutter just before his mouth took hers in a kiss that stole her breath away.

Epilogue

It appeared that every person living in Grady Gulch had turned out for the town festival. People thronged Main Street, which had been shut off to traffic, and colorful tables and displays appeared along the sidewalks.

It was just after ten when Nick and Courtney arrived on the scene with Garrett firmly locked down in a stroller. The air smelled of cotton candy and freshly baked pies and popcorn, making Nick's mouth water in anticipation.

For Nick this was more than just a town festival. It was also a celebration of the love he and Courtney had rediscovered, a love that was out in the open, there for all to see and one he knew would allow the dreams they'd once made in the shadows of the old barn to come true.

He grabbed her hand as he pushed the stroller with the other hand. She looked more beautiful than he could ever remember, wearing an emerald-green sleeveless blouse and white shorts that displayed her long, slender legs. Her hair was in soft waves to her shoulders, and the small smile of a satisfied woman curved her lips.

And he was a satisfied man. Although officially she was still living at the motel, for the past week she and Garrett had been at the ranch house, filling the emptiness with laughter, breathing new life not just into the structure itself but also into Adam.

Nick had two surprises today for the two people he loved, and when the time was right he'd give them both. But at the moment, as they walked down the street, greeting people left and right, he was simply happy to be beside Courtney and with his son.

The first place they stopped was at the stand Mary had set up to sell slices of homemade pie. The café was closed for the day, and she had Junior Lempke beside her as she sliced and sold pie, with the money being donated to a local charity.

"Ah, there you are." Mary greeted them with a bright smile. "I was hoping to see the three of you together today."

Courtney smiled at Nick. "Together today and every day."

"That's wonderful," Mary exclaimed and then frowned. "But, does that mean I'm going to be losing another waitress?"

"No, I'm still planning on working, at least part-time for a while," Courtney replied. She and Nick had discussed the issue, and Courtney had insisted she still wanted to work at the Cowboy Café. Nick could take care of Garrett when she was at work, and she promised she'd work only part-time.

"And now what I want is a piece of your cherry pie," Nick said and then looked at Courtney.

"None for me right now," Courtney replied. "I'll have a piece later in the day."

Mary sliced him a big piece and he gave some of the crust to Garrett, who smacked his lips for more.

From Mary's stand they moved on down the street, stopping occasionally to visit with people they passed. Cameron and several of his deputies stood on one of the street corners, looking official as peacekeepers.

The two murders of the waitresses hadn't been solved, and Nick knew the crimes weighed heavy in Cameron's mind, in his heart. But, today was a day to celebrate life, not contemplate murders, and he hoped at least for a little while today Cameron could put the murders behind him and just enjoy himself.

As they started past the booth the bank had set up offering free bottles of water, Grant stepped out from behind the table. Nick tensed as the handsome man approached them.

"Nick…Courtney." He greeted them with a smile.

Nick fought the impulse to throw his arm around Courtney and like Garrett exclaim, "mine!". "Grant, how's it going?" he asked.

"Good," he replied. "I have a feeling we're going to be handing out a lot of bottled water today."

"It is another hot one," Nick said.

Grant looked at Nick and then to Courtney. "The three of you look good together, like you belong together," he said. "I'm happy for you." He offered Nick another smile. "I just borrowed her from you for a little while."

It was obvious Grant meant what he said, that he'd moved on and harbored no grudge toward Courtney. "Thanks," Nick said and held out his hand. The two men shook and Nick felt as if another door of closure had occurred.

Garrett pointed with excitement in the distance as he saw Rusty Albright with a handful of balloons. Grant went back to his work behind the water table and Nick and Courtney moved on.

Within minutes Garrett had a balloon tied to his stroller, and as they approached the booth that Daniel and Lizzy were running, Nick felt the muscles in his stomach clench in anticipation, even though he'd been treated warmly by them at the Cowboy Café.

The booth was the carnival game of darts and balloons on a wall. On the right side of the backboard was a basket of stuffed animals, silly hats and fancy plates to be won with the burst of a balloon.

"Step right up and try your luck, cowboy," Lizzy said, her eyes sparkling in amusement. "Break a balloon and get a prize."

Courtney giggled. "You sound like a real carnival barker," she said to her friend.

Daniel looped an arm around Lizzy's shoulder. "She's a woman of many talents."

"See if you can win a prize," Courtney said as she grabbed Nick's arm.

Once again Nick's stomach muscles tightened with tension. Everything was in place, and he suddenly felt as if his entire life was on the line. All he had to do was break one balloon.

"Come on, Nick. You get three darts. Surely you can make one of them count," Daniel said.

Nick nodded and stepped up to the counter. "Watch Daddy, Garrett," Courtney said from behind him. "He's going to win us a prize."

Daniel laid three darts in front of Nick, and as he

picked up the first one a trickle of nervous sweat slid down his back. It was ridiculous to be so nervous. One way or another he knew he'd be a winner. Still, at the moment all he wanted to do was pop one balloon.

He was vaguely aware of a small crowd forming behind them. The first dart went far left, smacking into the side of the backboard inches from any of the colorful balloons.

"Ah, we have a novice with the darts," Lizzy exclaimed amid a few good-natured catcalls behind Nick.

Nick picked up the second dart and glanced at Courtney. Her grin warmed him from head to toe. She was his very heart, as was Garrett.

As he thought of that moment when Courtney had confronted her mother, his heart swelled in his chest. After that visit, they'd talked about her feelings for her parents, and he knew she realized that there was something broken inside them, something that would probably never be fixed.

"Hey, brother, you gonna throw that dart, or are you waiting for the A team to step in?" Adam's voice called from behind Nick.

Nick grinned at Courtney, then turned and let the dart go. It found its mark in the center of a bright red balloon that popped. The crowd cheered and Courtney threw herself into his arms as Garrett clapped with excitement even though he was too young to understand what was going on.

"Do I get to pick the prize?" Courtney asked, eyeing a cute teddy bear with a blue bow.

"Actually, when you break a red balloon the prize is preselected," Lizzy said, a bright, knowing twinkle in her eyes.

She bent down beneath the counter and pulled out the

tiny black cowboy hat Nick had arranged to be there. "Oh, Garrett, look!" Courtney exclaimed.

"Hat!" Garrett exclaimed.

A blue ribbon was tied around the hat and instead of handing it to Nick, Lizzy held it out to Courtney. "If I were you I'd take a good, hard look at that ribbon before I put that hat on your son's head," she said.

Courtney frowned at her as she took the hat. Nick knew the moment she saw it, the sparkling diamond ring tied to the ribbon. Her gaze shot to his in stunned surprise.

Nick took the hat from her trembling fingers and quickly untied the ring and allowed the blue ribbon to float away on the hot breeze.

With the ring in his hand, he fell to one knee. Courtney's eyes opened wide as the crowd of people began to clap and cheer. "Courtney, I love you," he said, shouting to be heard above the others. "Would you please make me the happiest man on the planet and marry me?"

Courtney's head bobbed up and down as tears began to race down her cheeks. "Yes." He saw her lips whisper the word. "Yes!" she shouted and he rose, and as he placed the ring on her finger she laughed and cried at the same time as he wrapped her in his arms and kissed her.

"Okay, folks, show's over," Lizzy shouted. "And that's the last diamond ring coming out of this booth today."

As the crowd began to disperse, Nick reached down and grabbed Garrett from the stroller. Courtney plopped the little hat on his head, a hat identical to the one that Nick wore.

"Mine!" Garrett said as he reached up to grab the rim of the little hat.

"Mine," Nick repeated and reached up to touch the brim of his own hat.

Garrett nodded and pointed to Nick. "Dada's hat."

Nick gathered Courtney into his empty arm. "Mine," he said as he held his family in his arms.

"I love you, Nick," Courtney said. "I can't wait to marry you and be your wife forever."

"I have everything I need in life." He took her lips with his, and in their kiss he tasted the bright joy of their future together. "I have the woman I have always loved, will always love, and my little cowboy son. What more could a man want?"

Courtney smiled, her green eyes twinkling with happiness. "A little cowgirl daughter," she replied.

* * * * *

REQUEST YOUR FREE BOOKS!

2 FREE NOVELS PLUS 2 FREE GIFTS!

◆ Harlequin®

ROMANTIC
SUSPENSE

Sparked by Danger, Fueled by Passion.

YES! Please send me 2 FREE Harlequin® Romantic Suspense novels and my 2 FREE gifts (gifts are worth about $10). After receiving them, if I don't wish to receive any more books, I can return the shipping statement marked "cancel." If I don't cancel, I will receive 4 brand-new novels every month and be billed just $4.49 per book in the U.S. or $5.24 per book in Canada. That's a saving of at least 14% off the cover price! It's quite a bargain! Shipping and handling is just 50¢ per book in the U.S. and 75¢ per book in Canada.* I understand that accepting the 2 free books and gifts places me under no obligation to buy anything. I can always return a shipment and cancel at any time. Even if I never buy another book, the two free books and gifts are mine to keep forever.

240/340 HDN FEFR

Name	(PLEASE PRINT)

Address	Apt. #

City	State/Prov.	Zip/Postal Code

Signature (if under 18, a parent or guardian must sign)

Mail to the **Reader Service:**
IN U.S.A.: P.O. Box 1867, Buffalo, NY 14240-1867
IN CANADA: P.O. Box 609, Fort Erie, Ontario L2A 5X3

Not valid for current subscribers to Harlequin Romantic Suspense books.

Want to try two free books from another line?
Call 1-800-873-8635 or visit www.ReaderService.com.

* Terms and prices subject to change without notice. Prices do not include applicable taxes. Sales tax applicable in N.Y. Canadian residents will be charged applicable taxes. Offer not valid in Quebec. This offer is limited to one order per household. All orders subject to credit approval. Credit or debit balances in a customer's account(s) may be offset by any other outstanding balance owed by or to the customer. Please allow 4 to 6 weeks for delivery. Offer available while quantities last.

Your Privacy—The Reader Service is committed to protecting your privacy. Our Privacy Policy is available online at www.ReaderService.com or upon request from the Reader Service.

We make a portion of our mailing list available to reputable third parties that offer products we believe may interest you. If you prefer that we not exchange your name with third parties, or if you wish to clarify or modify your communication preferences, please visit us at www.ReaderService.com/consumerschoice or write to us at Reader Service Preference Service, P.O. Box 9062, Buffalo, NY 14269. Include your complete name and address.

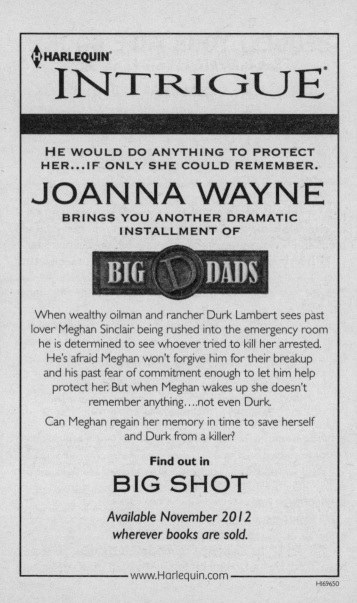

*Something's going on in Conard County's high school...
and Cassie Greaves has just landed in the middle of it.*

Take a sneak peek at RANCHER'S DEADLY RISK
by New York Times *bestselling author Rachel Lee, coming
in November 2012 from Harlequin® Romantic Suspense.*

"**T**here comes a point, Cassie, when you've got to realize that stuff you got away with as a child is no longer acceptable or even legal."

Linc paused, realizing he must seem to be going around in circles. Well, he probably was, between her damned scent and his own uncertainty about what was happening.

"I'll be honest with you," he said slowly. "I'm wondering what's been bubbling beneath the surface at the school that I'm not aware of. That makes me uneasy. On the one hand, I'm trying to paint it in the best light because I know these kids. Or thought I did. I don't want to think the worst of any of them. On the other hand, I guess I shouldn't make too light of it. There have been three transgressions we know about with you. Four, if we add James. I'm not going to dismiss it, but I'm not going to be Chicken Little yet, either. The mind of a teenage male is impenetrable."

She surprised him by losing her haunted look and actually laughing. "You're right, it is. And girls aren't much better at that age."

Girls weren't much better at any age, he thought a little while later as he drove her home. He'd certainly never figured them out.

"Thanks for a wonderful time," she said as he walked her to her door. "I really enjoyed it."

"So did I," he answered more truthfully than he would have liked. He had to bite his tongue to keep from suggesting they do it again.

She was still smiling as she said good-night and closed the door.

He walked back to his truck, keys jingling in his hand, and thought about it all, from the bullying to the rat to the evening just past. The thoughts were still rumbling around when he got home.

Something wasn't right. Something. He'd grown up here, gone to school here, been away only during his college years, and now had been teaching for a decade.

His nose was telling him something was wrong. Very wrong. The question was what. And who.

Find out more in RANCHER'S DEADLY RISK
*by Rachel Lee, available November 2012
from Harlequin® Romantic Suspense.*

HARLEQUIN *Blaze*™

red-hot reads

Double your reading pleasure with Harlequin® Blaze™!

2 GREAT NOVELS SAME GREAT PRICE

As a special treat to you, all Harlequin Blaze books in November will include a new story, plus a classic story by the same author including…

Kate Hoffmann

When Ronan Quinn arrives in Sibleyville, Maine, all he's looking for is a decent job. What he finds instead is a centuries-old curse connected to his family and hostility from all the townsfolk. Only sexy oysterwoman Charlotte Sibley is willing to hire Ronan…and she's about to turn his life upside down.

The Mighty Quinns: Ronan

Look for this new installment of The Mighty Quinns, plus *The Mighty Quinns: Marcus,* the first ever Mighty Quinns book in the same volume!

Available this November wherever books are sold!

HB79723